KOBA

KOBA

by

BOB BIDERMAN

LONDON
VICTOR GOLLANCZ LTD
1988

First published in Great Britain 1988
by Victor Gollancz Ltd,
14 Henrietta Street, London WC2E 8QH

© Bob Biderman 1988

British Library Cataloguing in Publication Data
Biderman, Bob
  Koba.
  I. Title
  813'.54[F]

  ISBN 0–575–04221–4

Typeset at The Spartan Press Ltd,
Lymington, Hants
Printed in Great Britain by St Edmundsbury Press Ltd,
Bury St Edmunds, Suffolk

To Joy Magezis
Friend, Comrade, Lover
And to those days
When all things were possible

Chapter One

Morris Kaplan, forty years of age though looking not much over thirty-five despite the thinning of hair in the region of his upper forehead (which was more than compensated for by the mass of unruly curls falling in tangles down the back of his neck), bearded out of obstinacy rather than desire, and not very caring that his blue work shirt still had a few stains from ancient meals, sat at his table in the Café Trieste sipping his second double espresso. He was mulling over an article in the crumpled copy of this morning's *San Francisco Chronicle* which he had found stuffed behind the pipes of the closet-like loo he visited on the stroke of ten with amazing regularity — as Yolanda, who had watched him come and go for the last fifteen years, could well attest.

What a copy of the morning paper had been doing stuffed behind the pipes was anyone's guess. Perhaps, thought Morris, some kind soul had left it there as back-up for the rather meager supply of sandpaper-quality tissue which hung stiffly on the roller bar. But, whatever the reason (if there was a reason), Morris was happy to have found an entire copy intact without having to wait like some hungry scavenger until one of the more flush clientele had finished with the morning rag and left it behind on a table, with the remnants of their coffee and brioche, for the likes of him. The problem was, there were too many of the likes of him hanging around these days. And too few gents who left their morning paper. So finding this one as easily as he had, without having to nearly snatch it from the hands of another bleary-eyed, print-starved vulture, was good news indeed. And if he had missed the article he was now perusing (which most people probably hadn't noticed since it was stuck under a lingerie ad on page fourteen), then he would

7

have taken the incident as an omen of something almost pleasant — perhaps the urban equivalent of finding a four-leaf clover.

He read the article twice through before putting the paper down on the crusty table and closing his eyes. It was then he realized how much his head still hurt. For the last few years it seemed as if his head always ached in the morning. It used to be that he had only needed a few sips of potent brew before that throbbing pain would subside. Then it had become a cup. Then two. Now he had to wait for a third. But cash was in short supply these days and with a good espresso reaching the price of a gallon of high-grade gasoline, it wasn't so easy to fill up anymore.

However, today it was not just a lack of caffeine that caused the ache in his head. It had more to do with the article, sitting so salaciously under the lingerie ad, headlined, in a matter-of-fact way, "Murder Victim Identified". And, as if the hundred odd words might have contained some mysterious revelation that Morris had missed the first two times around, he opened the paper and read them again:

"The victim of last Thursday's killing on Mullen Street in the city's Bernal Heights district was identified yesterday as Philip Lampam. Police Lieutenant Brian Murphy, in charge of the case, says no evidence of robbery has been found, nor has any other motive been established. This is the third ostensibly random shooting in Bernal Heights so far this year where the victim has been shot at his front door. Residents of the neighbourhood are angered at the apparent inability of the police to come up with any solid leads. Lieutenant Murphy said that the investigation is continuing."

Morris closed the paper once more and considered the notion that three people in a few short months had been shot at their front door for no good reason. The sheer irrationality was so horrific that he could hardly believe the story was relegated to page fourteen. Yet, he supposed, so many terrible acts of violence had passed under the metaphorical bridge since last Thursday, so many bludgeonings and rapes, shootings and stabbings, that a simple act of motiveless murder was starting

8

to seem, through the eyes of the press, like little more than spitting on the sidewalk.

Of course, to be fair, last Thursday, before they had discovered the victim had a name, the story had dominated the front page, with headlines screaming "ANOTHER RANDOM KILLING IN BERNAL HEIGHTS!" and "MASKED MURDERER STRIKES AGAIN!" But over the weekend there had been an earthquake in China, and three nuns had been found half naked in the Sierra Madres after losing their way during a torrential rainstorm (they had taken cover in a mountain cave and had been attacked by a grizzly bear). So the press had decided that monumental disasters of the raging inferno variety and raw adventures with a touch of sex and violence superseded, as far as sales were concerned, the notion of a loony bumping off innocent people in the comfort of their own homes.

He caught a glance of the clock above Yolanda's head, half hidden by the ornate bottles of Italian syrups and wines, before it and Yolanda, who was busily washing cups, disappeared behind a curtain of steam from the espresso machine as one of the new arrivals from Lombardy, who had been hired as a relief counter man, tried to foam up a pitcher of milk as the final step in constructing a near perfect cappuccino.

A brief shower that morning had driven a few extra people inside the café, so when Fredo finally arrived, Morris, who was seated toward the back, didn't see him at first. Then he noticed a large mass of dark, wiry hair under an Irish worker's cap bobbing up and down in the mass of people squeezed against the counter.

A confused face, sporting a modified Pancho Villa moustache and two bloodshot eyes, looked out from the crowd. A tired hand made a motion of recognition. Then, a heavy body, thickly set, plowed toward him.

"Thanks for coming," Morris said.

Fredo's dogged face was still wet from the morning rain. He shrugged and took a long drink from the white porcelain cup brimming over with foam, a goodly amount of which then stuck to his whiskers making him look even more like a haggard pooch. "What are friends for?" he mumbled. It was more a question than a reply.

"You've read it?" asked Morris pushing the *Chronicle* across the table. It was folded to page fourteen.

"I haven't had a chance to focus my eyes yet," said Fredo, taking another gulp of coffee before daring to lift the journal from its resting place. "I was up half the night," he said, as if he needed to explain. But he needn't have. Morris, too, had occasionally spent hours sitting at his desk, the words jammed up in his pen, as night crept on to day. "I can't seem to find an ending," he continued.

"Endings aren't that hard," said Morris. "You just put down your pen and stop."

Fredo blinked his eyes and looked at Morris as if pearls of wisdom had just been cast at his feet. "Why didn't I think of that?" he said.

Instances like this were extraordinarily frustrating for Morris. He could never tell whether Fredo had translated his sarcasm into some folksy aphorism straight out of the *People's Almanac* or whether he, in his own dry way, was being flippant back.

"Anyway," Fredo continued, putting on a brave face, "not to worry. I've got a teaching job next week. Things will sort themselves out then."

It had always amazed Morris how easily Fredo overcame his writing blocks. He might reach a snag, a point where the plot hit an impasse or where a character turned cardboard, but he didn't suffer over it long. He simply waited for an odd job to turn up, like substitute teaching, and then everything would connect. It happened all the time and it used to get Heather mad as hell.

"What do you think he does in the classroom?" she shouted indignantly when Morris had once brought the subject up with her. "How on earth can he write a novel there? I've been teaching for twelve years and I never had an original thought in my head during class-time. How can you with forty kids breathing down your neck, half of them zinging spit balls and the others crying bloody murder that they've been hit? I mean, really!"

10

Of course, Morris was a writer, too. He had one novel out entitled *May 68*. But it wasn't selling and he had used up his meager advance long ago. The book, which had been a culmination of some years' work, seemed to have disappeared out of existence. It had been such a dissapointment to him that he didn't wantn to be reminded of it anymore.

Fredo, on the other hand, didn't understand his problem. "Write another book," he had told him. "But this time write something that can sell. Forget about serious political fiction. There's no market for it in America. Say what you want to say, but put it in the form of an acceptable genre."

"Like mysteries?" Morris had asked him snidely.

"Why not?"

Fredo wrote detective stories. He had created an urbane, hard drinking, smooth opposite of himself by the name of Terrance LaRue. He gave his character some interesting backgrounds and then turned him loose. It seemed to work.

So Morris had tried his hand at several genre books. His best to date, at least in his estimation, had featured a detective who was a stumble-bum very much like himself, with a sidekick that was actually a monocled kangaroo. The problem was that in each of his attempts, somewhere down the line (usually by the third chapter), the book began to change into a story about the '60s. The characters refused to stay in their molds. They were undisciplined. They all seemed to have that anarchic flair which spoke of '68.

Therefore, in order to force himself into a disciplined mystery writer, Morris had started his own detective agency — more for research purposes than anything else. And as further inspiration he had taken to wearing a leather cap, just like the one he had seen atop the head of Bertolt Brecht in a photograph taken at the première performance of *Arturo Ui*, his play about the Chicago gangster scene.

Morris pushed the morning paper toward Fredo. "Read the article," he said, "and tell me what you think. It's right under the pantihose ad."

It was too early for even Fredo to be turned on by long bare legs (or perhaps it was the crease in the newsprint which made

11

the supple limbs look as if they had once been severed and then sewn, rather sloppily, back together), so he went directly to the article, trying to adjust the distance between the print and his nose so that the blurry smudges might form themselves into words. After a few minutes he put the paper back down and fumbled through his shirt pocket for a pack of cigarettes. "You got a smoke?" he asked, avoiding Morris' questioning gaze.

"Yeah," said Morris, taking a crumpled pack of Gitanes from his back pocket and handing it to Fredo. "I thought you took to calling them 'cancer sticks'."

Fredo withdrew a bent cigarette and smoothed it out. Then he leaned forward, allowing Morris to light him up. He inhaled deeply and, letting the smoke slowly drift out of his nostrils, said, "That was before I started again. You think it's Philip?"

"You think it's not?" asked Morris. He took the last of the cigarettes from the small blue pack before crushing it in his hand and tossing it into the ashtray.

"The city's probably pissing with Philip Lampams," said Fredo.

Morris shook his head. "I did a little detective work," he said almost proudly.

"You went to the morgue?" asked Fredo lifting his eyebrows, a sign that he found this a little hard to believe.

"I looked in the phone book," Morris replied, deciding, belatedly, that perhaps such mundane research didn't quite come up to Fredo's standards for hard-boiled private eyes.

"What did you find out?"

"That there's only one Philip Lampam listed."

"So what does that prove?" asked Fredo taking a puff from his cigarette and a sip of cappuccino. The coffee went down the wrong pipe and the smoke got lodged in his trachea, causing him to wheeze and gasp for air.

"Are you all right?" asked Morris.

Fredo held up a finger, like a drowning swimmer sinking fast. After a series of hacking coughs, which brought the café to an abrupt silence, he finally regained his composure and nodded for Morris to continue.

"It proves the town's not pissing with Philip Lampams," Morris said.

Fredo shook his head. "It proves the town's not pissing with Philip Lampams who list their number with directory information. If I were a Philip Lampam, I'd have an unlisted number too."

"You never liked him, did you?" said Morris.

"Who did?" Fredo replied.

Morris shrugged. "He was one of us once."

"Maybe," said Fredo, tightening his lips. "Maybe not."

"Anyway, we still have to find out," Morris insisted.

"I suppose we could call Mary," Fredo suggested. "She kept track of all the old people."

"The phone's over there," said Morris pointing to a booth stuck in a corner.

"You want me to call?" asked Fredo, not taking much pleasure in the notion.

"It was your idea," Morris replied. He didn't like phoning Mary any more than Fredo did because she always ended up reminding him about what he wasn't doing.

Fredo let out a sigh of resignation and got up from his chair. "You got a dime?" he asked. "I don't have any change."

"I'm a little short right now, Fredo," said Morris. "They'll give you change at the corner." And then, as Fredo turned to go, he said, "Get me a double espresso while you're up, OK?"

While Fredo was away on his mission, Morris found himself drifting back to those days almost two decades before — a realization that startled him since it still seemed only yesterday. There they were, as big and bold as life, sitting in the student café at San Francisco State College, dressed in their standard blue-jean uniforms – matching jackets and trousers complete with copper rivets, eating greasy fries and gagging on sugary milk shakes that Mary had acquired for them through sources which preferred to remain anonymous. The vision was so clear, he could almost hear the rhetoric ricochet off the sticky walls like verbal swipes in a hand ball game.

Morris smiled to himself. How easy it was to make fun of them now. They were so awkward, so young and inexperienced, so callow. And the task they had set out for themselves — to stop the Vietnam War, end institutional racism and, in the process, to bring down the ruling class all in one go — now seemed so ludicrous. But then — then revolution was in the air. And they had all been infected with the spirit of May '68 and its glorious motto: "All power to the Imagination!" Besides, thought Morris, what were they to do? Sit in their classes and let it all go on?

So there they were, at the long table, listening to Philip complain that he hadn't been consulted about some action they had planned, saying that he had been sick the day of the meeting and if he had a vote it would have all been different. And Fredo — good old Fredo — was saying that next time he should get a note from his doctor so that the revolution could be delayed till his sniffles subsided. And Philip, who by that time was beginning to foam at the mouth, was saying that participatory democracy meant that they had to wait for him — that's what it was all about. And Heather, rolling her eyes, said that the decision had been made and it was too bad. And Philip said that decisions could always be changed. And Roger said that decisions could only be changed if there was a pressing reason. And then Fredo said that he was late for class and he voted "no". And Philip, as confused as ever, turned to Heather and said, "What's he voting 'no' about? I didn't hear anyone call the question!" And Morris remembered choking with laughter, while Heather patted him on the back and Philip stomped off, seething.

"Here's your double espresso," said a voice. Morris looked down at the tiny cup with the fragrant black brew and then glanced up at Fredo, the contemporary version. "It was Philip, all right," said Fredo, sitting back down.

Morris felt his chest tighten. Having suspicions was one thing. Confirming them was quite another. "So we were mortal after all," he said, half to himself.

Fredo perked up his ears. "What's that supposed to mean? We all have to die sometime, Morris. Unless immortality was added to our list of ten demands."

14

Taking a sip of coffee, Morris stared at his old friend. There were lines in his face he hadn't noticed before. And, yes, even a few grey hairs. How come he hadn't seen them till now? "Remember how it was back then, Fredo? We never really talked much about it, but we were all prepared for some sort of violent end. Just thinking about revolution meant you had to consider it. But now . . ."

Fredo undid the cellophane from the pack of Camels he had purchased along with the espresso and offered one to Morris. "Death is death, Morris. You think a bullet is more violent than cancer?" he asked, lighting up.

"Cancer is more understandable than what happened to Philip."

Fredo shook his head. "Not to me it isn't." Then, looking down at the table, he said, "I half expected it, you know."

"What do you mean?" asked Morris.

He hesitated a moment, flicking the tip of his cigarette into the ashtray. Then he said, "The asshole had it coming to him." He said it calmly, without much emotion.

"You don't mean that," Morris replied.

"Like hell I don't! Who do you think was responsible for me spending six months in the county clink?"

"Not Philip."

"Not Philip my ass! The little turd handed me the billiard balls, didn't he?"

"Well why the hell did you take them from him? He didn't stick a gun to your head. Lots of people got caught with stuff when they busted us — pocket-knives, can-openers . . . you could always explain having things like that in your possession. But how do you explain billiard balls?"

Fredo, who had become quite heated, suddenly stopped as if it were all coming back to him. "Imagine spending six months in jail just for attending a campus rally!" For a moment, he looked as if he was once more in San Bruno jail, digging up weeds with a short-handled hoe.

"Well, you have to admit, it was a great way of getting us all in jail. Just declare a rally illegal and then bust everyone who attends."

15

"But at the Free Speech Platform in the middle of the campus?"

"Listen, Fredo, it was your idea to put up a political defense. Most of the other seven hundred of us just spent a couple of weeks in the can."

"Actually, it wasn't that bad," he said, with a slight cringe. "It sort of gave me a perspective on things."

"Perspective was in short supply back then," Morris agreed.

"What galls me," said Fredo, gritting his teeth, "is how that turkey got away scot-free!"

"You call being murdered at your front door getting away scot-free?"

"Back then I mean . . ." Fredo replied, realizing the absurdity of his remark. "Anyway, Morris, that's what I was trying to say. There's a whole line-up of people who wouldn't have minded sticking it to him!" Then, in a more subdued voice, he continued: "I don't think it was a random killing."

Morris furrowed his brow. How could Fredo know, he wondered? Perhaps he had also gotten the phone call. He half thought of asking him, but he didn't want to give away his cards too soon. So he simply said, "Why do you think that, Fredo?"

"Because I don't believe in accidents, Morris. If there's one thing that the '60s taught us, it's that nothing is accidental."

"What hat are you wearing now? Theologian or detective writer?" asked Morris, feeling the growing pain in his head.

"Think about it, Morris." Fredo was warming to the idea. "It's almost the perfect crime!"

"Come on, Fredo!" Morris said with a nervous laugh. "Are you trying to tell me that someone would bump off two innocent people in Bernal Heights just to make it look as if Philip was a random victim of insanity?"

Fredo shook his head like a tutor who had just failed his best pupil. "Why have I spent the last month trying to teach you the rudiments of crime? I've told you before, Morris, you have to learn to think like a criminal if you want to understand their actions."

"It just doesn't make sense," said Morris, somewhat defensively.

16

"But you're not looking at it in the right way!" Fredo replied in frustration. Then, leaning forward, he said in a conspiratorial tone: "Think about it, Morris. What if you wanted to bump Philip off and you'd been waiting, patiently, fifteen years for the right opportunity. You've kept track of his every move. You know where he lives, where he works, what he eats for breakfast. You're just waiting for something — you don't know what — just something that seems right."

He paused for a moment. There was a strange gleam in his eyes that made Morris' head ache even more. Fredo leaned closer and continued: "Then one day you read about some nut who's bumping people off in Bernal Heights just for jollies. He's already shot two and everyone's primed for a third . . ."

Suddenly it was quiet. The two friends just stared at each other. It was as if Fredo's hypothesis, crazy as it was, actually began to make sense.

Then Morris said, "Do you remember a guy named Koba from back then?"

Fredo's expression had become severe. The name had obviously conjured up something inside of him. "Sure," he said. "How could I forget?"

"Well," said Morris, "he's back in town."

Chapter Two

It was something after eleven that morning when Fredo dropped
Morris off at his cottage in the Noe Valley district, while Fredo
himself continued to Bernal Hill where he was doing a survey of
the shrubbery as "color" material for his next detective story.

"You're going to have LaRue sit on a hill and pick flowers?"
Morris had asked as Fredo pulled up before the old Victorian
house which shared the lot with Morris' tiny abode.

"There's nothing wrong with having a sensitive private eye,
Morris," Fredo responded. "Some people like that. I think I'm
going to make him an expert on exotic flora."

"Why not have him start with the back seat of your car?"
Morris pointed to the array of molds which had taken root in the
frayed upholstery. "There's no telling what amazing things he'd
find there. In fact, Fredo, if you ever want to do away with
anyone, you might just give them a ride through town with the
windows shut."

Fredo turned around and inspected the green garnish on the
rear seat as if he had never noticed it before. "You know," he
said, rubbing his chin, "that's not a bad idea. I think I'll use it
someday."

"Goodbye, Fredo," said Morris, getting out of the old jalopy
and shutting the door, "see you tonight."

"Right," Fredo replied, gunning his engine to keep it from
stalling. "I'll pick you up about eight." And with that he drove off
into the late morning mist which still awaited the brief afternoon
sun.

Morris opened the rickety gate and walked up the path which
led through Arnold's garden to his little two-room cottage.
Arnold was the owner of the property as well as the tender of the
garden which he farmed with a loving mixture of Bach recordings

18

and midnight snail hunts. Arnold was also a postman. He woke at four in the morning (about the time that Morris went to bed), delivered his mail, and was home by two in the afternoon. In his spare time, besides tending his garden, he practiced various "human growth potential" techniques which usually boiled down to screaming in cork-lined rooms or having his backbone hammered into shape by a variety of white-coated Amazons.

"Can you really afford this plantation on a postman's salary?" Morris had once asked him.

"I do a few things on the side," Arnold had said. "Are you in the market for some great hashish?" And when Morris had shrugged, Arnold had said, "I also have some Mexican sinsemillia that will blow your mind!"

"I don't want my mind blown, Arnold," Morris had responded. "I have enough trouble keeping it in place as it is."

This morning Arnold was in his garden hoeing the weeds as Morris made his way up the garden path.

"No mail today?" Morris said, by way of greeting. "The government run out of stamps or did people just run out of things to say?"

"That will never happen as long as we keep holding elections. Do you know how many thousands of pounds of bullshit I've carried up hills in the last couple of weeks?" said Arnold, putting down his hoe and wiping his brow with a polka-dotted neckerchief which he kept in the top pocket of his shirt. "Not to mention all the free samples of sanitary napkins and underarm deodorant. You don't know how embarrassing it is to slip a box of Tampax into the mail slot of a ninety-year-old pensioner who once earned his living laying track for the Union Pacific Railroad."

"So how are the kids?" asked Morris, trying to change the subject. He looked down at the rows of ripening vegetables. Arnold loved his plants the way some people love God. There was definitely a religious fervor in his voice when he spoke about them.

"Fine. They're doing just fine, Morris. The carrots are especially succulent this year after I sweetened the soil with a little lemon grass. And the tomatoes should be red and juicy by next week if we manage to get any more sunshine. If not, I think I'll bring out my tanning lamp for a while . . ."

Morris looked closely at his landlord as Arnold went on and on about the firmness and suppleness of his vegetables. He obviously got some strange, erotic thrill from plants. In fact, Morris wouldn't have been at all surprised if Arnold had a pin-up picture of a celery stalk in his bedroom. Then, again, at least he wasn't asking him for the rent.

"So what are you doing home today?" Morris asked, after Arnold had finished giving him a complete run down of the progress of each species growing in his plot. As he waited for a response, he lit up one of the Camels he had borrowed from Fredo earlier that day and had stuck in his shirt pocket for later.

Arnold watched him with dismay. "It's my day off," he said. Then, unable to keep his feelings inside, he added: "You know, you shouldn't smoke that stuff. It's not good for you."

"Tobacco's just another vegetable, Arnold," said Morris, flicking an ash into the breeze. "And it's the only one that doesn't give me loose bowels." Sometimes looking at Arnold's ruddy complexion and sleek hair, washed, he was sure, with some herbal shampoo like Flower of Muskrat, made Morris sick to his stomach.

"But you'll die of cancer if you keep on smoking like that!" he chastised.

Morris gave him a hard look. "And what will you die of, Arnold?"

"Die?" The idea, obviously, had never occurred to him.

"Arnold, did you ever consider that there are more important things in life than having a healthy head of hair?"

Arnold was becoming flustered. "What's wrong with having nice hair, Morris? Do you enjoy having dandruff?"

"I'm talking about priorities, Arnold, of which yours are questionable."

"Like not asking you to pay the rent?"

Suddenly, Morris realized that he may have gone too far. "That's one of your better qualities," he said. "And I do appreciate that you aren't a typical money-grubbing landlord, Arnold."

Arnold waved his hand in a gesture of conciliation. "That's OK, Morris. Even though I could get $800 a month easy for your place and even though I've got to make $147,000 this year . . ."

Morris looked at him suspiciously. "You have to make $147,000 this year? How come?"

"It's one of my goals, Morris. I want to be a millionaire by the time I'm forty."

"I see," said Morris, nodding his head.

"But I don't want to do it by being a greedy landlord."

"That's very commendable of you, Arnold," said Morris, edging sideways.

"Besides, I know you'll pay up when you sell your next book."

"You can count on it, Arnold," said Morris with a forced smile.

"Hey, Morris," said Arnold, bending down and pulling a carrot out of the patch, "no hard feelings. Have one of these."

"No thanks, Arnold," Morris said, continuing to edge toward the cottage door.

Arnold lovingly brushed off the dirt from the orange root. "It's OK," he said. "It's organic."

Morris shook his head.

"Come on, Morris," he insisted, "take a bite. It won't hurt you. It's just Ruthy the Carrot. She's swell!"

"You name your carrots, Arnold?" Morris narrowed his eyes.

"Sure. You name your books, don't you?"

"Yeah, but I don't eat them."

"Well, I grew her from a seed. She's special. That's why I'm giving her to you."

"You want me to eat a carrot named Ruthy? Arnold, you're not well!"

Both Arnold and the carrot looked truly hurt.

"I'm sorry, Arnold. Can you replant her?" Morris said apologetically.

Arnold got down on his hands and knees and scooped out a bit of dirt from where he had taken the carrot. "I'll try, Morris. If she dies it will be from a broken heart, not because the roots were torn."

Morris suddenly found that he was feeling sorry for the carrot, despite himself. "My God!" he thought. "Is this what it's come to?"

Meanwhile, Arnold had patted the soil back in place around

Ruthy and was now upright again. "Don't worry," he said, a smile once more on his face. "She'll be OK." It was hard for Arnold to stay angry for long. "By the way," he continued, "there was someone nosing around your place today."

"Nosing around my place? What do you mean, Arnold? Was it Heather?"

"No. It was a guy . . ."

"Fredo?"

"No. This guy was pretty straight looking. Wore a suit. You're not in trouble with the cops, are you Morris? I mean, with my sidelines I really can't take any chances . . ."

"Was he blond?"

"I couldn't tell, Morris. He was wearing a hat. Do you know who it was?"

"It's probably a bill collector, Arnold. The cops haven't wanted me for the last fifteen years."

"What should I say if he comes back and asks me about you?"

"Say that I moved, Arnold. Just say that I've moved."

"Oh, one more thing," Arnold called out after him. "There was a delivery for you."

Morris glanced back at his landlord. "A delivery?"

"Yeah, I put it on your mantelpiece. Who's Bubbles?"

"What bubbles are we talking about now, Arnold?"

"What a card you are, Morris!" Arnold said with a chuckle. "It's really great having you around!"

He found them on the mantelpiece, just like Arnold had said, arranged in an old milk bottle as Morris didn't have a vase. There was a card attached with a bright red ribbon. The message was written in a feminine hand; it read: "Darling, I love Puccini as much as you. See you soon. Yours forever, Bubbles."

He sat down on the bed. Someone's strange idea of a joke, he thought, but the flowers did brighten up the room. He wondered why he had never thought of putting flowers on the mantelpiece before. Perhaps it was that no one, up till now, had ever sent him any. Heather always had flowers in her flat. It made her place smell like spring.

Morris lay in bed thinking till just after noon. He was definitely troubled. Fredo was right about one thing, of course. There were few of them who would mourn Philip's death. But Philip had been with them in the thick of things, when the world was ablaze and everyone had been forced to choose sides. He had chosen the same side as them, and even if he had been difficult at times — well, hadn't they all? How could they have withstood the hatred of the others, who didn't want their lives disrupted no matter how many bombs were being dropped on Hanoi, without having been "difficult"?

On the other hand, Fredo had brought up something he hadn't considered. Philip had started to back off from them just as things were getting tough. Where was he during the trials? Hadn't he conveniently disappeared? There had been talk, he remembered. But there was always talk when people backed away. He never believed Philip was a stoolie or a spy. Philip wasn't the type. Then, again, who was the type? Still, one thing was certain: Philip was dead. And even Fredo didn't think it was an accident. No, they knew better than to believe press reports of random shootings. If the press were to have been believed, then they themselves would have been petty criminals set on mob violence. Their actions would have been as senseless as firing a gun through an open door. Fredo was right. There was no such thing as an accidental murder.

Morris looked at his watch and then got out of bed. He went over to the sink in the tiny bathroom and doused his face with cold water. He looked in the mirror and studied his image. He was no longer sure he liked what he saw. Maybe the answer was to wash his hair with Flower of Muskrat shampoo. Sometimes he was no longer certain at all.

He made a vain attempt at brushing back his flyaway hair and then, giving it up, returned to the all-purpose room and put on his jacket. But who would want to kill Philip, he wondered? What had he done? And then he thought of Koba. Why was he back? Why did he telephone?

He went to the front window and peeked out to make sure the coast was clear. Seeing no one in the garden, he opened the door and quickly went down the path to the gate.

23

His office was only five minutes down the street. When Curtis had refurbished the old butcher shop and turned it into a café, Morris had suggested that the huge walk-in refrigeration-room would make a great place for him to hang up his shingle: "Morris Kaplan, Investigator".

"What the hell's an investigator?" Curtis had asked him. "A private eye?"

"In my case 'public eye' would be more appropriate, I think," Morris had replied.

"I thought you were a writer," said Curtis.

"Well, you have to investigate things before you write about them, don't you?"

"So what are you going to do if a client comes along and wants to hire you?"

"That situation hasn't arisen yet."

"But what are you going to do if it does?"

"I'm taking a wait-and-see attitude, Curtis."

"What does that mean?"

"It means I'll have to wait and see."

He and Curtis had both driven hacks for Yellow Cab after the docks had shut down, but Morris had been canned by the Teamsters after he tried to set up an opposition faction of cabbies.

Curtis had been saving all his dough to buy a café and couldn't see the point. "They're all crooks, Morris, the bosses and the union, but you can still make a bundle if you play your cards right. Why do you want to mess around with politics?"

"It's in the blood, Curtis," he had said. "I just don't like seeing people getting screwed."

"Well, it's your life, man," Curtis had shrugged. "But the Teamsters play hardball."

Morris didn't last more than a couple of months, but others took over the fight and carried on a campaign that culminated in a long and tortuous strike.

"So what did you accomplish?" Curtis asked him some years later.

"Maybe nothing," said Morris. "But there's no reason not to have tried."

The old walk-in refrigerator had become the back room of the café. Unfortunately, Curtis removed the top half of the walls so that the division from the main room was just a boundary line. But worse than that, from Morris' point of view, he had hung a "No Smoking" sign. Nonetheless, Morris took the back room over as his office, preferring not to work at home during daylight hours, despite the fact that customers would often barge in uninvited.

Today his office was, thankfully, empty when he arrived. But he hadn't been there more than ten minutes, writing up some notes, when Rosa stuck her head through the opening, which once had been the door where the carcasses passed through on their way to cold storage, and wagged her ponytail to get his attention: "Hi, Moishe!"

Rosa called Morris "Moishe" because Heather called him by that name. And Heather called him "Moishe" because once, during a quick trip back East, she had met his grandmother, a great and beautiful Russian woman who had fought in the October Revolution, and she had called him that.

"Hi, Rosa," Morris said, glancing down at his watch. "I thought you'd still be in school now."

She came over to the table and plopped herself down on an adjoining chair. "Nope. It's a holiday today."

"A holiday?" He looked at her questioningly. "How come the streets aren't full of kids if it's a holiday?"

"It's just for my school," she said, looking him straight in the eye without flinching. Half of him hated that she could lie so well; the other half quite admired her for it.

"Does Heather know?" he asked.

"Heather doesn't have to know everything!" she said, wrinkling up her nose.

"Heather is your mother," said Morris.

"And you're my dad. So what does that prove?"

"When it's my year to take care of you then I'll want to know where you are too."

"Otherwise you don't care, right?"

"Of course I care! What do you think I'm asking you for?"

"Probably because you want to work and you're annoyed that I'm here."

25

He ran his fingers through what remained of his hair and considered her words. She was certainly an expert at wringing out whatever residual guilt remained in him — an emotion which he found quite annoying — so he launched his first line of defense: "How about a hot chocolate? You want a hot chocolate?" he asked, reaching for his wallet.

"I'm not asking for a bribe," she said, looking up at him with her bright green eyes.

"OK," he replied, starting to put his wallet back in his jacket pocket.

"But I wouldn't refuse."

He sighed and looked through the contents of his billfold. Not much remained from the ten spot he had gotten for the last box of used books he had sold. "How much is a hot chocolate these days?" he asked.

"It's gone up to a buck, I think," she said. "You sure you can afford it?"

"Sure," he said. "What are dads for?"

"Well you don't look so good, Moishe. Like you haven't been getting enough to eat. Why don't you come over to Heather's and let me make you a peanut butter sandwich?"

"I don't like peanut butter."

"How about a banana."

"I'm all right, Rosa," he said with annoyance. "Food doesn't really do much for me anymore." He took out the last of the freebies Fredo had given him and lit up.

She looked at him in horror. "Moishe! This is a no smoking area!"

"I won't tell if you won't," he whispered.

"But, Moishe! That's not nice!"

Morris closed his eyes. "Rosa, do you remember who you're named after?"

"Don't you know? After all, you named me!" she said, giving him one of those looks.

"Actually, it was Heather who named you, but never mind. I just want to know whether you remember."

"Rosa Luxemburg," she said with a groan.

"And how did she die?"

"With a smoke in her mouth, singing the *Internationale* as she was getting beat over the head by a bunch of Nazi thugs. I've heard the story before, Moishe."

"Yes, well the important point is the smoke-in-the-mouth bit. Anyway, be thankful you're not called 'Moonchild' or 'Lysergic D'."

"I knew a kid in my school named 'Sotweed'," she giggled.

"His parents should have been shot!" said Morris. "Don't you like the name 'Rosa'?"

She shrugged. "It's OK. I don't know what I think about being named after someone who was bumped off . . . Can I ask you something, Moishe?"

"You can ask me anything, Rosa. You know that."

"Will you and Heather ever get back together again?"

"We get together — occasionally."

"I mean, are you ever going to move back in?"

"Is that important?" he asked. "We still see each other."

She shrugged. "I just thought that if you moved back in then maybe you wouldn't have to hang out in dumps like this all the time."

Morris looked around. The Meat Market was a little ratty, but it was a contained rattiness that had been built into the place since it opened. "I sort of like it here," he said, turning back to her. "It reminds me of the '60s."

"Moishe, everything reminds you of the '60s." She pointed to his clothes. "Look at your jeans. You don't even have stitching on the pockets. Don't you feel embarrassed?"

"Wait around a while, Rosa. It'll come back into fashion again."

"And look at your hair. Men aren't wearing it long anymore. You look like one of those guys. You know. The Bugs." She started to giggle.

"You mean the Beatles. Rosa, do you know how expensive haircuts are?"

"So let Heather cut it for you. I'll even cut it if you want."

"Rosa," he said, covering his eyes with his hand. "Do me a favor . . ."

She gave him a pouty look. "Just trying to help, Moishe."

27

There was something he was going to reply. It was on the tip of his tongue, but it wouldn't come out. "Here," he said, handing her a dollar. "Go buy a hot chocolate."

She hopped out of her chair with a gleam in her eyes. "Thanks, Moishe!" she said. "I'll be back!"

"Is that a threat or a promise?" he muttered to himself.

He tried to get back to work, but somehow all the brilliant ideas that had been floating around in his mind before she had intruded had evaporated — poof! — into thin air. He found himself sketching a picture. He didn't know what it was at first, but soon it became a portrait, a portrait of a man. Then he recognized the face. It was Koba. The tiny pencil dots had become Koba's piercing eyes. He drew in a jagged line on the forehead, where he remembered Koba's scar.

Rosa had come back with a cup full of chocolate. She put it down, clumsily, on the table, splattering some drops of brownish goo over Morris' papers.

"Look what you've done to my picture!" Morris said in a mock angry voice.

Rosa leaned over. "Hey, I know that face!" she said.

Morris suddenly felt his heart skip a beat. "You do?" he said in a low voice. "When did you see him?"

"Just now," she said.

He looked at her seriously. "Where, Rosa?"

She gave him a strange look. "Why right here, Moishe. Isn't that a picture of you?"

Morris left her in the café, still sipping her cocoa, with the excuse that he had some important business that couldn't wait.

"With your publisher or a client?" she had asked.

He couldn't tell whether or not she was being sarcastic. There were times when he saw her as just a miniature version of Heather: same eyes, same hair, same innocent righteousness that made him end up feeling even more guilty and annoyed.

The Noe Valley district where Morris lived had once been a quiet lace-curtain Irish neighborhood with a sprinkling of German shopkeepers. However all that had changed when the Haight-Ashbury had burst its boundaries, like an overfilled balloon, spilling hippies, students, beats and lefties into the far reaches of the city.

Morris had arrived in the early days when there were still just a few of his kind who listened to Dylan and lived like Bohemian castaways among the aborigines. But it hadn't been long before the cheap rents attracted the flock. By then 24th Street had already begun to change as the cobblers and small grocers and knickknack shops that sold tacky little porcelain dingies, along with Hallmark greeting cards ("To Mom on Housewife's Day"), made way for bookstores and espresso cafés. For a while it was the place to be, like the Village in the '20s or North Beach in the '50s. And Morris felt, at last, he had found a home where he and Heather and Rosa could settle down.

But then something happened to make it all turn sour. He wasn't sure when it started, but one day the realtors arrived and sold the area like it had never been sold before. And suddenly, a two-bedroom house with creaking timbers and ancient plumbing, which had overlooked the city from Noe Hill since the time of the great earthquake and been home for a progressive assortment of butchers, bakers and other tradesmen, became the trendy symbol of professional success, quadrupling in value overnight. It meant, in Morris' estimation, that the day of the hip bourgeoisie had finally arrived. But where did that leave him?

Often, now, when Morris walked down 24th Street, he would curse each quiche and chocolate truffle shop that had burrowed into the neighborhood, fervently wishing they would move back to Nob Hill or Pacific Heights or wherever they had come from. He ached for the return of a simple hot-dog stand that sold greasy french fries and root beer. But today, as he quickly strolled down the avenue, his mind was on other things. And if a new hair salon, named Fifi's of Paree, was opening that moment, he couldn't have been bothered to let out a groan.

Café La Bohème, where Morris was headed, lay at the bottom of 24th Street hill just as it leveled out into the flatlands of the Mission District. Here the French cheeses under fancy awnings were exchanged for simple tacos and beans. Yet even this Latino sanctuary had not been exempt from the plight known to urban sociologists as "gentrification" but which Morris referred to as "bourgeoisicide".

The corner of 24th Street and Mission, where La Bohème was located, exemplified the mischief. A few years before it was the hub of the Latin community. Then came BART, the Bay Area Rapid Transit system, which was built simply to woosh the middle classes into the city from the suburbs and then woosh them home again. In its wake, the small shops which sold plantinos and chilies were replaced by clones of Kentucky Fried Chicken. But the spirit of the area remained — for Morris, at least — on a wall which faced the barren landscape and had been taken over by the *muralistas*. It was a picture of workers, done in the mestizo tradition of Diego Rivera, holding the tracks of BART aloft, while the sleek trains filled with suburbanites rolled mindlessly along.

Café La Bohème was filled with the lunch-time crowd when Morris came in. Not long ago there would have been no problem at all finding a seat. But that was before the place had taken off. Back then it was the home for the fringe theater and dance people who were located in the top-floor garrets of crumbling neighborhood buildings. Now it provided soup and salad for the shoppers.

Ed was working the counter that afternoon. He was one of the owners who had been lured by the romance of the Continental café, not realizing that even he would fall prey to the perils of the entrepreneurial disease.

Ed's red beard was drooping when Morris finally made his way to the top of the line. "Morris, I haven't seen you in a dog's age!" The weariness in Ed's eyes seemed to fade.

"Well, it wasn't much of a pup," said Morris. "How's business?"

"Too good," said Ed, waving his hand toward the madding crowd. "I look back fondly to the days when I was broke."

"That also has its disadvantages. How about standing me to a cup? I'm a little short right now."

"One of these days you'll grow again, Morris. You're a good writer. I read your book."

He knew there was an excellent reason why he liked Ed.

Perhaps this was it. "Listen, was there anyone here asking for me?" said Morris.

"You mean your fan club? They must meet in another café."

Morris grimaced. Well, there probably was another reason, he told himself. "A guy in his forties. A little taller than me. Muscular. Blond."

"I got 'em any shape and any size. How many you want?"

"I don't want any," he said. And then, suddenly noticing a window table opening up, he grabbed his coffee. "Thanks Ed. I'll pay you when my new book comes out."

"Sure thing, Morris," Ed called after him. "Don't mention it."

A window seat at noon was a prime find at La Bohème and Morris wasn't going to let it pass, even if it meant blocking out two legitimate paying customers. It was the law of the jungle in this place. Sit or be sat on.

"Excuse me," said a young man, balancing a bowl of soup in one hand and a roast beef on rye in the other. "Is that seat taken?" He nodded to a vacant chair at Morris' newly acquired table.

"Yes," said Morris.

"But I don't see anyone sitting there," insisted the young man.

"He's in the head taking a piss," said Morris curtly.

The young man wandered off. Morris wasn't usually that proprietary, but today was special. He was waiting for someone and he wanted their conversation to be private.

He had gotten the phone call late last night.

"Hello," he had growled, "who the hell is it?"

The voice on the other end had sounded fuzzy. He couldn't make out the name.

"Speak up! It's past my bedtime!"

"Koba," came the hoarse reply. "You remember? State College, 1968 . . ."

He recalled the name, but not the voice. And sitting now at La Bohème he thought back to those days and remembered:

It was night. He was at Koba's place on Alma Street, right off Stanyon, on the edge of the Haight. Koba had poured him another glass of Greek retsina and Morris was beginning to feel his head spin.

31

They were sitting in Koba's tiny kitchen at a wooden table that was held up by three legs and a column of books. In the sink was a stack of dishes with scraps of chili starting to turn green. Opposite, the ancient refrigerator had a marking pen dangling from a magnet. The door was covered with revolutionary slogans scribbled in emphatic handwriting : "*Avanti! Viva la communista! Libertad!* Arm the people! Take up the gun!"

Koba's eyes were ablaze as he spoke of the coming revolution. Beads of perspiration dripped from his brow as he told of the rising of the proletariat and how they would march triumphantly on City Hall to raise the red flag. It was, he said, just a matter of time. Not decades, not years, but months. The time was right. The time was now! And it was up to them to lead it.

He stopped and looked at Morris and smiled. "Are you with me, Morris?" he asked.

"I don't know," Morris had replied. "Revolution is serious business. I'm not sure we're ready yet."

"No one's ever ready for it," said Koba, grabbing Morris' wrist and squeezing. "But it happens, Morris. It happens. And, Morris, the moment is here. The question is whether we dare . . ."

There was a strange look in Koba's eyes as he spoke. Morris remembered feeling a moment of terror and pain, as if Koba's grip would break his wrist in two. When he finally let go there were red impressions where his powerful fingers had been. The man was mad, he remembered thinking. But so was revolution. Yet isn't that what they had all wanted?

Then Koba had leaned forward and smiled again. "They sent you here, didn't they?" he asked.

"What do you mean?" Morris had replied, rubbing his arm. His heart had stopped for a moment.

"Tell me the truth," said Koba.

He remembered thinking what an ass he had been. Why did he let them put him up to it? He hadn't the temperament to be a spy. So he admitted it. "Yes," he said. "They wanted to find out about you."

"What will you tell them?"

"That you're crazy but sincere. I don't think you're a cop."

Koba's smile had widened. "How do you know, Morris?"

He hadn't. But what was he to say?

Later that night he had given his report when they had gathered at Mary's flat.

"He's an adventurist," said Morris. "He's ready to arm the workers and start the revolution."

"That's a good way to get yourself shot," said Fredo.

"The only way to arm the workers in this country is to take them duck hunting," muttered Alice.

"That's a load of crap!" said Bert. "Just try tampering with their color televisions and see what happens."

"Come on," Roger had said. "What happened to the worker-student alliance?"

"It's on strike," said Bert.

"Shut up and let him finish his report!" Philip had shouted. And then, turning to Morris, he said, "Is he a Trot?"

"Judging from his bookshelf he's read everything from Bakunin to Mao. Trotsky and Stalin stood side by side between Hoxha and Lenin."

"Literate little bastard, isn't he?" said Jeffery.

"He's not so little," Fredo put in.

"So what do you think?" asked Philip. "Can he be trusted?"

"The question could just as easily be asked of us, Philip," said Fredo.

"That's horse shit!" said Philip. "I'm getting sick of your cynical attitude, Fredo!"

"And I'm getting tired of your patronizing mouth!" Fredo had shot back.

"He says he can get us twenty automatic rifles," said Morris.

"What do we want with twenty automatic rifles?" asked Heather.

"We could set up a shooting gallery at the next Students for a Democratic Society carnival," Fredo suggested.

"How about trading them for twenty canisters of laughing gas?" said Alice.

"Now let's be serious for a minute," said Roger. "We shouldn't be too hasty about turning him down . . ."

Heather had stood up and screamed, "Are you going batty,

Roger? We're trying to organize students to protest the war, not form suicide squads!"

"There's no need to yell, Heather," Philip said calmly. "We're not talking about using them."

"If you want toys, Philip, Woolworth sells them cheaper," Fredo said.

"We're thinking of the future, Fredo," said Roger. "But I agree, this probably isn't the time or the place."

"Damn right!" said Heather.

"You know," said Philip, "with that attitude you're not going to be much use when they open up the camps."

"Are you trying to tell me that twenty rifles are going to stop them from opening up the camps, Philip? Is that what you're saying?" shouted Heather.

"I went to camp once when I was ten," said Fredo, turning to Morris. "It wasn't so bad."

The words came through to him as clearly as if they had been spoken yesterday, not years ago. And as he heard them in his mind, he cringed. Were those really the people who were going to make the revolution, he wondered? But then he thought, if it wasn't them, who would?

Last night, however, the conversation had been brief.

"I need to talk to you," Koba had said.

"Talk," said Morris. "I'm listening."

"Not on the phone. Can you meet me tomorrow at that place on 24th and Mission?"

"La Bohème?"

"Yes. Two o'clock. Can you make it?"

"I'll try," said Morris, regretting it even then. And that was it. Koba had hung up.

Morris looked down at his watch. It was ten after two. The young man who had wanted the seat walked past. "Your friend still pissing?" he asked snidely.

"He saves it up. He only pisses once a week," said Morris, getting up to go. "Last time he was in there for the entire day."

Outside La Bohème the sun was bright enough to blind a snowman coming from a deep freeze. Morris had to stop a moment in order to adjust his eyes. The street was crowded with shoppers and people going back to work after a late lunch, as well as the others — the ones who were always there, the bag ladies and the young hangers-out with bottles in their paper bags and needle holes in their arms.

A man he had never seen before came up to him and stopped. He was dressed in tattered clothes, ragged even for this district. His black hair hung in tangles and he looked as if he hadn't shaved for a week. The man didn't say anything. He just stared. There was something about his eyes that Morris found intriguing — like a drowning swimmer lost in a sea of despair. Morris automatically reached into his pocket and searched for some change. Finding none, he made a motion with his hands — a universal movement which said more than words could ever say. In response, the man took a plastic flower from his own pocket, leaned forward, and attached it to Morris' lapel.

At that moment a bus which had just pulled alongside the curb began unloading passengers who pushed their way past with the determination of a truckload of cattle being let off at an abattoir. An elderly woman passing by was jostled in the fray and had dropped her grocery sack. Morris bent down to pick it up. He handed it to her and saw her brown, wrinkled face light up with gratitude.

It happened in a flash. Morris had heard the sound — a crack and then a hollow thud. But he took no notice. It was a street sound, that's all. A street sound — like a backfiring car or a hissing beer-can. He turned to see the ragged man disappear into the mass. It was then he became aware of the gathering crowd, silent, filled with gruesome curiosity, circle around him in a voyeuristic ring. He looked down and saw the old woman lying in a pool of blood oozing from her chest.

Chapter Three

The cop at the desk looked down and grinned in a way that would have put warts on a frog. "You never seen a dead body before?" he asked.

Morris had been sitting on a wooden bench in the Mission cop house about an hour now. For most of that time his face had been in his hands. It was a reasonable question, he thought. Forty years old and still a virgin. Maybe it was some kind of a record.

"That's the trouble with you punks who never went to Vietnam. If you done your duty, maybe you'd be a man by now."

"How do you know I'd never been to Vietnam?" asked Morris, looking at the cop through splayed fingers.

"'Cause you look like one of them creeps who used to shout 'Make love not war' on the ten o'clock news."

"Actually, I think I was shouting 'Bring the war back home', if I remember correctly."

The cop's face had darkened; his jaw sagged for an instant as if an invisible hinge had been released. Morris suddenly felt like a rabbit on a highway caught in the glare of an oncoming juggernaut. This was one of those situations where he knew he couldn't win. He could only hope the conversation stayed rhetorical.

"You know what you are?" asked the cop.

"Sometimes," said Morris. "Sometimes not."

"You're the commie–liberal slime we got to walk through just to do our job! The only thing you shits are good for is fertilizing weeds! I wish all you creeps was six feet underground!"

"Well," Morris replied, "things are looking up for you. I hear that soon every cop is getting supplied with a horse, a mask and some silver bullets again."

Now that the fuse was lit the cop at the desk was set to explode. The only thing that saved him was the bell.

The cop picked up the phone at his desk. He listened, placed the receiver back down and then glanced up in a way that put a few more warts on Morris' hide.

"A friend of yours wants to see you, Kaplan . . ."

Morris looked confused. "A friend of mine? Here?"

The cop pointed with his pencil over his shoulder. "Down the hall. Third door to your left. Lieutenant Murphy. Homicide."

Lieutenant Murphy used to work out of central headquarters at a place Morris and his crowd had dubbed "The Hall of Injustice". Back in the days when the world was ablaze, Murphy was head of what was not-so-euphemistically known as "The Red Squad". It had been his job to keep track of people like Morris, Heather and Fredo, even if, in the end, that didn't give him much to do. So, like others in his profession, he was often called upon to use his imagination. Just how fertile was Murphy's fantasy life hadn't been truly appreciated until the Mother Joneses finally laid hands on their files through the Freedom of Information Act. They had spent a few evenings laughing at the incredible conspiratorial world Murphy had created, until it dawned on them just how serious it might have been. Filtered through time and the various bureaucracies, fed into computers, transmitted by modems, lies had become truth, honor had become betrayal, and innocence had become a grotesque form of villainy. Innuendo and slander had become part of their official bio-graphies. But even so, only Heather had been outraged enough to demand they try to take it through the courts in order to get their records expunged. No one else believed it could be done.

Morris stood before the door marked "Homicide". He hesitated. What went through his mind that moment was an image from many years before:

It was late at night. He and Heather had been walking home after one of those interminable caucus meetings. They had taken no notice of it at first — it was just another squad car on patrol. But as it crept along behind them at a snail's pace, Morris felt a chill run down his spine. He grabbed Heather's arm and tried to hurry her along. But Heather pulled away in a huff, saying they had a right to walk the streets no matter what the time and she wasn't going to be bullied by the cops.

They had reached a block of Guerrero where the streetlights had been blown out by kids with B-B guns. Somehow, as they passed an alleyway, he knew it was coming: there was that sensation, that feeling, like the unpleasant heaviness in the air before a storm. Suddenly he heard the squeal of tires. In an instant the squad car had lurched onto the sidewalk, blocking their way. The doors swung open and two cops got out.

They didn't need an introduction. Murphy had been around for some time; he knew them all by name.

"Hello, Kaplan," Murphy had said. "Taking your dog for a walk?"

He looked different that night. When they had seen him before, during the day, he had been almost polite, occasionally allowing himself a little smile as he took his copious notes. Now even Heather found it difficult to find anything to say outside an angry glare.

It was the first time he had experienced that sense of terror, of total powerlessness, confronted on a dark night at the entrance to a lonely alley by two men with guns who could do anything they liked.

Murphy's sidekick walked up to Heather and grinned. She told Morris later how she had smelled his whisky breath. "What do you see in that creep?" the cop had asked, reaching out and grabbing one of her breasts in his meaty hand and squeezing it hard enough to hurt. "I bet he's never given you a decent fuck."

"Get your filthy hands off me, you pig!" she hissed.

As Morris watched, feeling himself grow nauseous, Murphy came up close to him — so close that Morris felt the metal tip of Murphy's boot weigh down on the toe of his shoe. "Ain't you gonna do something about it, Kaplan? It seems to me my friend's molesting your woman. I don't think I'd let him get away with it if I were you . . ."

He couldn't help looking into Murphy's eyes. He felt the hatred and fury well up inside of him. But what he felt most was the fear.

"I can take care of myself!" snapped Heather, breaking free from the cop. She went over to Morris and grabbed his hand. "Come on," she said, "let's go! They've got no reason to stop us like this!"

He let her pull him along. Every moment he expected to feel the sharp heat of a bullet in his back. He couldn't believe they were letting them walk away like that. But they did. He heard the raucous laughter through the silence of the night. And echoing in his ears was Murphy's shout: "Hey, lady! Don't forget to change his diaper when you get home! He's leakin' through his pants!"

At home that night Heather undid her blouse and saw the marks upon her chest and had finally let herself go. Then it was like the crumbling of a wall of steel; and once her defenses were down, once the tears began to flow, it all surged out in salty waves of pent-up furies and suppressed fears.

Morris had tried his best to comfort her, but, really, his mind was trapped in those moments just before: they had dared him to make a move, and though he hadn't fallen for the bait he couldn't help but wonder what he would have done if she had actually been raped. It provided the meat for a series of terrible nightmares which lasted for many years thereafter.

Morris knocked on Murphy's door. He waited a minute and then he knocked again.

"Enter!" The voice itself made him quiver.

It was one of those rooms that smell of formaldehyde just because it looks as if it should. The place had the feel of a morgue. Morris wouldn't have been surprised to have found a few dead bodies tucked away in the closets, not out of subterfuge but simply because they were there and no one knew what else to do with them.

Murphy was seated at a desk behind a pile of papers. At another desk was a plain-looking woman with the drab of civil service oozing from her face. She held a stenographer's notebook in one hand with a pencil at the ready. A man in a white laboratory jacket stood by the side looking extremely bored.

"Sit down Kaplan!" Lieutenant Murphy pointed to a straight-back chair.

Morris sat.

"Still hanging out on street corners, huh, Kaplan? You handing out leaflets? Or maybe you're into dealing drugs these days?"

"I ran out of leaflets about ten years ago," Morris replied. "And you know I wouldn't deal drugs."

"Well, times change, Kaplan. People change. And, as they say, we all gotta earn a living." Murphy looked hard into his eyes. "How do you earn yours?"

"Not very well."

"I don't doubt it. Did you know the lady, Kaplan?" Murphy kept staring at him.

"The old lady who got shot?"

"I wasn't talking about your wife." He smiled. "How is she these days, Kaplan? Still suffering from sore tits?"

Morris turned to the secretary. "I hope you're taking all this down . . ."

The secretary glanced at Murphy. Murphy shook his head and she rubbed something out.

"I got a witness who says you bumped into the deceased and made her drop her stuff. Is that right?"

Morris shook his head.

"What happened?"

"People were getting off the bus. She got caught in the crowd and dropped her shopping bag. I picked it up."

"Sir Galahad, huh?" Murphy snorted.

"Wouldn't you do the same?" Morris looked at him and then figured he probably wouldn't.

"I got another witness who says you were chatting with a pretty disreputable-looking character right before the old broad was shot. True?"

"A tramp came up to me and tried to hit me for a hand-out. That's all."

"How much did you give him?"

"Is that relevant, Murphy?"

"Maybe . . ."

"Go stuff yourself!"

Murphy's expression began to change. His smile had a hint of the sadistic. "Why'd you shoot her, Kaplan? Seems she had three grandchildren and one more on the way. If you wanted to bump someone off, why didn't you take out one of your own kind? Nobody would miss 'em . . ."

Morris felt the drummer in his head begin to pound "You know I didn't shoot her, Murphy. Furthermore, I bet you know that she wasn't the intended victim."

"No? Who was the intended victim then?"

"I don't know. Maybe me . . ."

"You? And I always thought you were such a nice guy. Who would want to bump you off, Kaplan?"

Morris glared at him. "I thought you knew everything, Murphy."

Murphy turned and nodded to the man in the white laboratory jacket who took a tray and walked over to where Morris was seated.

"Hold out your hands," he said.

"What?"

"Hold out your hands," the lab man repeated.

"Go to hell!" Morris snapped. Then, looking back at Murphy, he said, "I'm calling my lawyer."

"Suit yourself, Kaplan. You can either submit to the test or call your lawyer and spend the night in the clink. It's up to you."

Morris thought for a moment, let out a sigh and held out his hands.

"Palms up," said the lab man.

He held his hands out, palms up, and the lab man swabbed them with a solution. Then he inspected them closely and let them drop.

"All finished with your games?" asked Morris.

The lab man went over to Murphy and said something in a hushed voice. Murphy entered a notation in a file.

"Can I go?" asked Morris, standing up.

Nobody said anything to him as he went to the door, opened it and walked away.

It was late in the afternoon by the time he made his way to the neighborhood library on Jersey Street. He did a quick bit of research and then walked down the road to Fredo's house on Sanchez Street.

41

Fredo lived in a basement flat under a chiropractor's office. To reach it one had to climb over various rubbish bins that the other tenants placed before his door. There was no bell. Fredo didn't particularly like unexpected visitors. If you wanted him, you had to beat, loudly, on the window-pane.

"I thought I was picking you up at your place," Fredo said when he finally opened the door.

"I figured I'd save you the trouble since I was in the area anyway."

"It wouldn't have been any trouble," said Fredo. And then, hesitating, he finally said, "I suppose you want to come in?"

"Just for a moment," said Morris. "I really need to talk to you. It's not inconvenient, is it?"

"Not in that way," said Fredo. "I was just in the middle of an experiment," he said, leading the way inside.

"An experiment?" Morris repeated. It always took a moment to adjust his eyes in Fredo's underground chamber. The dankness and lack of sunlight would have satisfied Dracula.

Fredo pointed to a fish bowl with a piece of cellophane over the top. "I caught a mouse this afternoon and I decided to see what would happen to it if I locked it up with some of the mold from the back of my car."

Morris looked at him with amazement. "Why do you want to do that?"

"Well, it was your idea, Morris. If it croaks, I'll send the stuff to the lab for analysis. Maybe it'll be the basis for a new mystery."

"Fredo, I think that mold has already rotted your brain."

"It's more than my brain that's being rotted," Fredo replied. Then, realizing something else was on his buddy's mind, he said, "What's up?"

Morris rubbed his eyes. "Something happened today . . ." he began.

"You saw Koba?"

He shook his head. "I saw a woman get shot . . ." He stopped to gauge Fredo's reaction.

Fredo was nervously twisting his moustache. "Where?"

"On 24th and Mission. Right outside La Bohème."

"Did you know her?"

"No. But she was standing about as close to me as I am to you. She'd dropped a grocery bag. I'd bent down to pick it up."

"You're lucky whoever shot her had good aim," said Fredo.

"No one was trying to shoot her, Fredo! She was just an old lady!"

"You mean old ladies are exempt?"

He stared at Fredo with wild eyes. "Are you nuts? I went there to meet Koba! Do you understand what I'm saying now?"

"I understand that you're upset," said Fredo, still playing with the hairs above his lip.

"They pulled me in for questioning," said Morris, a little calmer after his outburst.

"The cops?"

"Murphy."

Fredo had grown distinctly pale. "I need something to eat," he said, grabbing his jacket. "Let's get out of here."

The Chevy was parked just a short walk away from Fredo's underground pad. They got in and drove down Sanchez, making a right on 24th Street and a left on Valencia. Just as they reached the corner of 16th Street, Fredo slammed on the brakes with a force that almost threw Morris into the windscreen.

"Sorry," Fredo apologized, putting the car into reverse. "I saw a parking space and I don't want to lose it."

One of the neighborhood alcoholics, who was propping himself up against a lamppost after having taken a much needed leak in the adjoining alleyway, tried to help guide them into place, waving his arms madly as if he were bringing down a B–29 bomber.

"'Er ya go, jus' a wee bit more—oops, too much. Be'er back off a bit. Asss a way, fella. Now a l'll up. OK! Mash it! Oh, oh . . ."

Fredo's Chevy was just a few inches longer than the space allotted to it. But having once parked cars for a living, Fredo knew that with a couple of expert fender-crunching maneuvers he could get his tank into any space that didn't shove back.

The other denizens of the street, the parched-throat mob who dotted these alleys and stoops and waited like inebriated taxi dancers for someone to offer them ten cents a dance, looked on expectantly. So when Fredo had left the Chevy and, out of habit, tossed the drunk two bits, a sea of calloused, sweaty hands stretched out to them as they walked toward their destination.

"Don't look back," said Morris.

"I never look back," said Fredo.

"I mean one of those guys is washing your car, but you wouldn't want to see what he's using for a hose."

"Don't tell me," said Fredo. "I've got a good imagination."

"Might kill the mold though," said Morris.

The Café Picaro sat opposite the old Roxie theater which, in days gone by, had been the haunt of down-and-outers with a few bucks to spare who wanted to see a pair of breasts, if only on a short clip of sixteen millimeter film. Then, as the area began to change, drawing students and artists from the high-rent neighborhoods around Dolores Park, the place was taken over by a group of cinema buffs who wanted someplace to screen the collected films of Salvador Dali, undeterred (and perhaps even stimulated) by the smell of stale urine. To the surprise of all, when they opened the doors of the "new and unrefurbished Roxie" there was an anxious audience waiting to get inside (though whether it was to see the film or to get away from the panhandlers Morris never knew).

The Picaro opened soon afterward. It was managed jointly by a Spaniard and an Irishman, one fat and the other thin. Each day the Spaniard made the fresh gazpacho soup which stood on the counter in a clay urn. The Irishman sat at a table and bought cartons of books from destitute intellectuals (like Morris) who were down to their last sou. These books were then placed randomly on the shelves which lined the walls of the café. You could read at your pleasure and then purchase or not, depending on your desire. At first Morris thought this was like trying on a coat for the winter and returning it in the spring. But the more he thought about it, the more he decided that the Spaniard and the Irishman had really hit on something: a company store for the bohemian intellectual. Here was the only place in town they could trade a book, when times were tough, for a coffee and a fag and then buy it back again (for twice the price) when things were a little better.

"You want a bowl of gazpacho? asked Fredo as they walked up to the counter.

"Just coffee," said Morris. "I'm on a diet."

Fredo gave him a quick up and down. "Come on," he said, "you have to eat. Anyway, I'm buying." Then, signaling to the woman behind the counter, he said, "Two gazpachos, please, Carla."

The woman behind the counter smiled exotically as she ladled the cold cucumber soup into bowls. She moved like a dancer, with artful steps and graceful hands that barely touched the spoon. Her hair was jet black, like a panther, and she had a figure as lithe. Her features were gentler, more like a kitten, complete with almond eyes.

"What do you think?" asked Fredo as they settled down at a table stuck away in a corner.

"Is this a general knowledge question or are you referring to something specific?" Morris replied.

"About her," said Fredo, nodding back toward the woman at the counter.

Morris took a spoonful of the gazpacho soup. There was nothing he hated more than cold vegetable soup except, perhaps, warm vegetable soup. Then, looking up, he studied her body with a practiced eye. "Very nice," he said.

"Did I tell you that she's Basque? She came to San Francisco with a flamenco group and then decided to stay. The Spaniard gave her a job."

"The Spaniard has better taste in women than he does in soups," said Morris taking another spoonful and making a face.

"You don't like it?" asked Fredo, with surprise. "This stuff's the real thing."

"Well, real or not, it's giving me indigestion. You have a cigarette?"

Fredo handed him his pack of smokes. "How long have you been off solid food?"

Morris shrugged, took out four cigarettes (three of which he put into his shirt pocket), handed the rest of the pack back to Fredo and then lit one up. "I get a hamburger at Doggy Diner every now and then. It's hard to keep it down, though."

"You ought to see a doctor, Morris."

"Why? He'd only tell me what I already know. And charge me for it, besides."

"What do you know?"

"That I live off nicotine, java and whisky – when I can afford it."

Fredo sighed. "I guess I don't have much of an appetite either."

"I thought you said you were hungry."

"Not anymore. I think your paranoia is rubbing off on me."

"Paranoia?" Morris shook his head. "I thought you were the one who didn't believe in accidental deaths!"

"Not every bullet's aimed at you, Morris, even if it does come close. I bet if you looked around at 24th and Mission you'd find hundreds of spent cartridges. I bet there's a shooting on that corner every night."

"This was in the middle of the day . . ."

"How long did they keep you at the police station?"

"A couple of hours, I guess. Murphy was trying to put the frighteners on me."

"Why?"

Morris shrugged. "I don't know. Maybe he's just a sadist. Maybe it was for old times' sake. There were a million witnesses around. Nobody found a gun. Nobody saw her shot." He looked at Fredo questioningly. "Why would a lab guy paint my hands with a swab?"

"They were looking for traces of gunpowder."

"What would have happened if there were?"

"Probably change color, I guess."

Morris inspected the palms of his hands.

"You didn't shoot her, did you Morris?"

"No. But I don't trust tests. I bet every third person who gets the chair is convicted because of a test that went wrong."

"I suppose that's what most paranoid people would claim," said Fredo. "What did you do when they let you go?"

"I went to the library."

"Makes sense. Check out any of my books?"

"I thought you said they were all stolen, Fredo."

"That's right. I steal 'em myself and then have the library order new copies. I just wondered whether they had come in yet."

Morris took out his notes. "I tried to locate the articles about Koba's arrest."

"Yeah, I remember he was busted. But I can't remember what he was busted for . . ."

"He was indicted for selling guns to the Black Defense Army. Calhoon was his lawyer."

"Rocky Calhoon who defended us in the Mass Arrest?"

"Yeah. He got him off. Then he was busted again. This time on a drugs charge."

"I thought he was a dealer!" Fredo said emphatically.

"Well, they were always picking people up on phony drugs charges back then, Fredo. Anyway, he jumped bail."

"And was never seen again."

"Till now, anyway."

Fredo took a spoonful of gazpacho and let out a burp. "I suppose it is a coincidence him turning up like this just when Philip is bumped off."

Morris looked at his friend. "Think about it, Fredo. Philip is shot, ostensibly by a madman. Koba calls me for a meeting. Then an old woman is killed for no apparent reason and she just happens to be standing next to me. It's got to be Koba . . ." He rubbed the side of his face. "I just don't understand what his motive would have been."

"Maybe Philip squealed to the pigs about the gun thing. We all knew Koba was trying to unload some weapons. Maybe he suspected you as well."

Morris shook his head. "But why wait all these years?"

"I told you, maybe he was waiting for the perfect time."

"That doesn't sound like the simplest explanation, Fredo."

"What's your theory then?" Fredo asked him.

"Remember the Lowenstein murder?"

"You mean that congressman who used to be down at Stanford? He was killed by some nut, wasn't he?"

"Lowenstein was a political heavy who was active in the Freedom Rides in the early '60s — remember when everyone was going down South, Fredo?"

"I didn't go, but I remember seeing the marches on TV. You couldn't tell the cops from the Ku Klux Klan."

"Yeah. They both were capable of stringing you up from a tree. One of Lowenstein's students at Stanford went down there with him — a kid named Sweeney. Seems he was busted and while he was in jail he was beaten senseless. Then he dropped out of sight. Some years later, when Lowenstein had been elected to Congress, Sweeney reappeared one day and shot him. He claimed the CIA had stuck transmitters in the fillings of his teeth in order to control his mind."

"So you think Koba's a lunatic out to destroy his political past?" said Fredo.

"What do you remember about him?" asked Morris.

Fredo thought a bit. Then he said, "I remember the incident with the jocks when we tried to get the military recruiters off campus."

Morris closed his eyes and recalled the time the Army, Navy and Marines had joined forces and had spent the day out on the campus lawn seeing how many students they could entice into trading their scholarships for a two year stint in Vietnam. Their little group, the Mother Jones Caucus of Students for a Democratic Society, had decreed, in the famous words of La Passionara, that "they shall not pass" (though "pass" to them meant passing out jingoist literature on their campus green).

It had been one of their sillier adventures. And it was Heather who had talked them into doing it. Heather was very artsy-craftsy and she had taught them how to make origami flour bombs.

"Some of this bleached flour on their fancy uniforms is just like egg on their faces. It injures their pride. They'll slink off in disgrace!"

Unfortunately, someone let the cat out of the bag (could it have been Philip, Morris wondered?) and when they arrived for their little agitprop, the recruiters were surrounded by the entire football team.

"It's just a play, fellas," Heather had shouted. "Relax, you might learn something."

"Looking up your skirt, sweetie-pie," one of the jocks had shouted back.

"You wouldn't know what to do with it anyway, buster!" Heather had replied in her own inimitable way.

The jock had begun to snort and hoof the ground. His team-mates had to hold him back for fear of starting the fracas too soon.

It was a short play. The men were the pilots. The women played the Vietnamese peasants. As the planes came circling overhead, the women fell to the ground, clutching their children to their breasts. Then, someone stationed in the audience shouted, "Don't bomb the peasants, bomb the recruiters. Recruiters off campus!"

And as the crowd took up the chant, "Recruiters off campus!", hundreds of flour bombs, like avenging pigeons, burst upon the starched uniforms of the military men.

To the jocks, it was as if their flag had been defiled. Enraged, they charged the players, hurling punches like jack hammers, lashing out like Wagnerian supermen who had witnessed their fair maidens' honor betrayed.

Though they had fought well, their little group was no match for these hormone-inflated bullies. In terms of brute force, they were definitely losing. But something happened that changed it all. One moment they were being hammered into dog meat and the next they were on their feet, watching the jocks retreat to the gymnasium, licking their bloody wounds.

"What happened?" Morris asked. "How did we get out of it?"

"Don't you remember?" Fredo looked at him curiously. "It was Koba."

And then it all came back to him. It was Koba, tall, strong, maniacal, swinging a baseball bat like a kid hitting fungos in the park. Except Koba wasn't a kid, he was older than them. And the balls he was hitting were, in fact, heads. The jocks, truly cowards at heart, took off like the fox who had been feasting on rabbit and then saw the hound. And those of them who could stand, watched it all with mouths agape.

"Did we ever thank him?" asked Morris.

"Thank him? For what?" asked Fredo. "We were doing all right for ourselves."

"Maybe," said Morris.

They both stared down at the table for a while, quietly lost in their own thoughts. Then Fredo got up. "You want a coffee?" he asked.

"Sure," said Morris. He let his mind wander over the ruins of former days till Fredo returned with a mug full of brew.

"Carla gets off at ten," he said. "She'll join us then."

"Who's Carla?" asked Morris.

"The Basque," said Fredo. "I asked her to meet us. I told her we were famous."

"Well, you'll have to be famous by yourself tonight," said Morris downing his coffee in several quick gulps. "I'm seeing Heather." And with that he rose from his seat and bid Fredo farewell.

He hadn't really made plans to see Heather that evening, it was just he needed to be with her tonight.

Outside, the drizzle had started up again making the bleak area even more depressing. The old Roxie theater looked squalid in the pale moonlight. The young man in the glass-enclosed ticket box was reading a comic book, his dirty shoes balanced on the ledge, oblivious to the debris of paper cups and used popcorn-boxes which, pushed by a relentless breeze, were piling up around his little guardhouse like flakes of urban snow.

Along Valencia Street, the drunks had taken refuge in the alleys, constructing shelters from the rubbish bins, and under the awnings of the shops. There was an evil smell which the rain had released. Piss and vomit, Morris thought: the telltale odors of abject poverty. For in each alley lay the wretched of the earth, huddled together for some trace of warmth or alone among the litter of yesterday's meals. It was a scene so familiar now that he was hardly aware it had entered his consciousness. And yet, the repulsion was there within him, stimulated by the dank and dreadful smells. The humans and the garbage had come together in a process of decay. And even he, who knew what poverty and depression meant, had a hard time differentiating them.

The sounds of Valencia Street at night were muffled in the quiet rain. The lights of cars, travelling fast, like cloistered cells, windows rolled tight, doors bolted shut, melted into the haze. His footsteps on the pavement had a hollow sound. And the shadow of his figure seemed to sink into the porous surface of the stone.

It wasn't till he reached the corner of 23rd Street that he became aware of a strange sensation. The feeling was in his spine and it worked its way to his feet making them sensitive to the weight of his body. There was a hot breath of air which surrounded him, heat from the rush of adrenaline, and it filled his nostrils with the scent of danger.

He stopped at the corner, under the flashing lights, took one of the cigarettes Fredo had given him and fumbled for some matches with an unsteady hand.

Heather had warned him that he would go through periods like this, when his nerves, poisoned by an excess of nicotine and coffee, would start to rebel, opening the locked chamber of his mind wherein were stuffed the terrors. He had paid her little heed because he had wanted to get in touch with something else within him, that spark of creative power, that special insight which had been so long represssed. And he knew from experience it was a delicate balance between realizing that creative force and giving in to paranoia.

But this evening, under the half-moon, filtered through the drops of rain, there was cause to be afraid. As he lit his cigarette, he had noticed a figure, not far behind him, emerging out of the mist and coming his way. The ghostly form, half hidden by the drizzle, had an aura of malevolence as it descended.

The Café Babar was only a block away and Morris quickened his pace. There he could have a glass of wine and wait it out. If it were a phantom, the alcohol would soothe him and make it go away. If it was a man, he would be safely inside. Out of harm's way.

The neon sign of the Babar beckoned in the darkness, pulsating sweetly like candy-coated veins in a technicolor sky. He could hear the man's steps behind him. They were heavy, firm, self-assured. The café was just a minute away. He found himself almost running toward the door. And then it struck him. The glass door was black. Inside the picture window, the chairs were empty. The café was closed!

Behind him the steps grew louder. He turned, half petrified, to face his accoster as the figure advanced toward him. "Koba!" he said, his voice hoarse with fear. "What do you want from me?"

The man had the collar of his raincoat pulled up around his neck. His wide-brimmed hat was bent down as protection against the rain. "Morris," he said, "don't you recognize me?"

Morris narrowed his eyes and tried to focus on the face which was now only inches away from his own. "You're not Koba," he said, betraying his confusion.

"Do I look like him?" asked the man. There was a smile on his face. Something about his eyes looked vaguely familiar.

"You're Jack!" said Morris in amazement, recalling the expression which he had known so long ago. "Jack Chesterton!"

"Yes," said the man. "Back from the dead!"

Morris turned and looked, nervously, up the block from where Jack's figure had emerged. Whatever other mysteries the darkness held remained a secret. He looked back at the man, his face still betraying his confusion and said, "I don't understand, Jack. What are you doing here? How did you find me?"

Jack hunched his shoulders and pulled his hat down on his head. "Do you mind if we walk?" he said, brushing the drops from his eyes. And without waiting for Morris to respond, he started off.

"I happened to see you in the café . . ." he said, looking over at Morris who was struggling to keep pace with his stride.

"You were there?"

"I had just come in when you left. I wasn't sure it was you. I followed you out. Called your name, but you were in another world . . ."

"How the hell did you recognize me?" said Morris. "What's it been? Twenty years?"

"At least twenty," said Jack. He turned and smiled. "You haven't changed."

"You must have though," said Morris. "After all those years in Vietnam."

Jack stopped at the corner, underneath a lamp. "I didn't go to Vietnam, Morris."

"You didn't?"

"It was someone else," said Jack. His voice sounded tense. "Morris, I need your help."

"My help? What can I help you with? I'm just one step away from the poorhouse, myself."

"It's not money," he said, suddenly breaking into a grin. "Have you ever known me to be short of dough?"

Standing there beneath the light, Morris saw Jack's face more clearly. It wasn't the thin, smooth-cheeked young undergraduate he had known in Berkeley. This was a rounder countenance, rougher hewn, with baggy eyes. But the smile, that seductive smile, filled with easy confidence, was just the same.

"So what's this all about, Jack?" Morris asked again, still not absolutely certain this vision was, in fact, real. "I mean I haven't seen you for twenty years and suddenly we're standing in the rain underneath the lamplight in the middle of the night and you're asking me for my help like we were bosom pals."

"We were," said Jack.

"Twenty years ago." Morris looked at him suspiciously. "What are you doing here, Jack?"

"Care for a smoke?" Jack asked, taking out a silver cigarette case from his jacket pocket and opening it up.

Morris shook his head. He made it a point never to accept cigarettes from ghosts.

Jack lit up and let the smoke trail from his lips like midnight fog. "I understand you're an investigator now."

"Not the sort you're thinking about," Morris replied. "I just use it as a front for my writing."

"I'd like you to help write something up," said Jack.

"Me? Why me, Jack? You can write . . ."

"It's not something I can write myself. Besides, I need an intermediary . . ."

"An intermediary?"

Jack looked over his shoulder again and then lowered his voice. "I've got an important story, Morris. A story that needs to be told . . ."

"Jack, what the hell is going on?"

"This isn't the place to talk," said Jack. "I'll get in touch with you later. I just wanted to let you know I was here." He winked and put his hand on Morris' shoulder. "Morris, it's really good to see you!" And with that, he turned and walked away.

53

"Wait a minute, Jack!" Morris called out. "You don't have my phone number. It's not listed in the directory!"

But it was too late. The figure had already disappeared into the night.

Chapter Four

It was just after midnight when Morris finally arrived at Heather's place on Elizabeth Street. He was still in a daze as he climbed the stairs leading to her door, so it took him a while to fully realize that his keys were missing.

Going around to the back of the house, he noticed that Rosa's bedroom window was partially open. He carted the rickety ladder from the shed, leaned it against the side of the building and made his way up the steps.

The curtains were fluttering in the night air as he climbed inside her room. Rosa was fast asleep in her bed, cuddled up with her favorite toy, an elephant which Morris had gotten her some years ago at a flea market. He had told her the floppy ears were like magic wings and each night at story-time she would listen eagerly, her eyes filled with wonder, as Morris took her on far-off adventures to marvelous places on the back of this ragged doll. But that was long ago.

A tiny night-light led the way through Rosa's cluttered room, but once inside the hall he had to feel around in the darkness. He was on his way to the kitchen when he bumped into the telephone table, toppling the phone and the directories onto the floor.

Rosa could have slept through the racket even if it had been the midnight locomotive coming through the hall instead of Morris. But Heather always slept with one eye open and when she heard the crash she leapt out of bed clutching the heavy pipe-wrench which she kept by her side.

Thrusting open the door, Heather barged into the hallway and advanced toward him, terrified, but resolved to save herself and her child from the intruder who so brazenly had forced his way inside. The metal wrench was poised above her head like a battle-axe. She looked, for all the world, like an industrial Joan of Arc, ready to slay the neighborhood dragon.

"Good God, Heather! It's me!" he shouted.

"Moishe!" she screamed, dropping the weapon and then, clutching her chest like the leading actress in *The Perils of Pauline*, "You scared the living daylights out of me!"

"Well, you almost turned mine out for good, Heather!" he shouted back. "What were you planning to do with that wrench?"

Heather wasn't in the mood to discuss the use of heavy metal objects with him. "I'd rather you slept off your late-night drunks someplace else, Moishe," she said, bending down to pick up the disabled telephone.

"I'm not drunk, Heather . . ." His voice sounded strange and rather pathetic.

Heather turned on the light. Seeing at once that he was in emotional trouble again, she let out a stoic sigh. "What is it this time, Moishe?"

"I had a run-in with Murphy today," he said, letting his gaze drop to the floor.

"Murphy? You mean the Murphy we knew from the Red Squad? What happened, for heaven's sake?"

He looked up. The name itself had been enough to gain her undivided attention. "An elderly woman was shot this afternoon outside of La Bohème. She was standing right next to me . . ."

Heather shook her head, trying to make some sense of what this was about. "I don't understand, Moishe. What are you saying?"

"I'm saying a woman was shot today for no good reason and I was standing next to her. Murphy called me in for questioning . . ."

He saw her wince. "Come on," she said, leading the way to the kitchen. "I'll make you some tea."

He followed her inside and watched as she put the kettle on the fire.

"What did Murphy want from you?" she said, making the tea and bringing it over to the table. She sat down beside him and looked into his eyes.

Morris shrugged. "I was the closest witness, I guess . . ."

"You were standing right next to her? You saw her shot?"

56

"I didn't see, exactly. I heard something that sounded like a shot. The next thing I knew this old lady was lying on the ground with a bullet in her chest."

"Was she alive? Did anyone try to help?"

"There were a couple of nurses in the crowd. They tried to do what they could . . ." He rubbed that spot on his head. "You know, Heather, I never saw anyone die before."

She stroked him, tenderly. "Poor Moishe. It must have been terrible for you."

"I wasn't the one who was shot," he said, taking the tea and giving it a stir.

"But you might have been . . ."

He felt a chill as he took a sip of the brew. He made a sour face. "What is this crap?"

"'Nighttime Delight'. It's a mixture of camomile, sassafras bark and hibiscus leaves. Don't you like it?"

"It tastes more like 'Hippy's Revenge'. Don't you have any coffee left?" he asked, taking out a cigarette and lighting up.

She looked at him reproachfully. "You're still smoking?"

"Yeah. You're still worried about the air, Heather? I thought you bought yourself a room-ionizer."

She got up, went over to the cupboard and took out a jar of freeze-dried Maxwell House. "I'm worried about you, Moishe. Besides, cigarette smoke seems to clog it up."

"Grass doesn't?"

"No." She brought him over the coffee. "It doesn't seem to."

"Maybe you're just too stoned to notice," he said taking a sip.

Heather sat back down, closed her eyes for a moment, and then opened them again. "I'm sorry, Moishe. I know it must have been awful for you. But I've got to be at Hunter's Point by eight tomorrow. That means I have to be up by six-thirty."

"You're teaching out at Hunter's Point?" he asked, taking another sip of the watery brew. Heather never had learned the rudiments of making a simple cup of coffee, he thought to himself. Even after all those years of living together.

"It's either that or Oakland. And I really detest the commute."

"I guess it's rough teaching there, huh?" he said, suddenly feeling a touch of sympathy for her.

"Yes."

"At least you're still teaching, Heather. You're a fantastic teacher."

"I'm not teaching, Moishe. They don't want teachers anymore."

"What do you mean?"

"I'm just a prison guard."

"A prison guard?"

"Yes. They just want someone to keep the children off the streets." Her lips were quivering. "I hate it, Moishe. I truly hate it."

"Then quit, Heather."

She didn't reply.

He got up and walked behind her and stroked her thick, auburn hair. "I'm sorry, Heather," he said. "I know it's my fault . . ."

She turned and looked up at him. "It's not your fault, Moishe. I've told you that before. I choose the way I want to live."

He put his hands on her shoulders, gently massaging her muscles. "Did you hear about Philip?" he asked.

She nodded. "Mary phoned. She wants to have a get-together or something."

"A wake?" asked Morris. He had finished massaging her shoulders, the way she had taught him to do, and had sat back down beside her.

"A wake or whatever," said Heather. Then, looking into his eyes she said, "I'm scared, Moishe. I don't know why, but I'm frightened."

He took her hand. It was like connecting up to a nostalgic time machine. For an instant he saw them the way they used to be, huddled together against the world, the heat of their passion at night blocking out the terror of the day. He brought her hand up to his lips and kissed it.

She smiled. She had the look of a gentle fawn, he thought, when she wanted to be loved.

"Can I spend the night?" he asked.

"I thought you already had," she whispered.

"No," he said, getting up and tugging at her hand. "The evening's just begun."

She allowed herself to be drawn toward him. Their lips touched the way they had a thousand times before. Each time different; each time special. His hands found their place on her thighs and then slowly began to draw the folds of her nightgown up to her waist.

Suddenly she gasped.

"What's wrong?" he said. "Too fast?"

"No," she said, stepping back a pace and putting her hand over her mouth. "I forgot to make Rosa's lunch!"

"Rosa's lunch?" he said unbelievingly. "Can't you do it tomorrow?"

"It is tomorrow, Moishe. If I don't do it now, I'll forget. I'm hopeless at six-thirty."

"Can't she make her own damn lunch? After all she's twelve years old!"

"She's ten. And if I don't make it, she won't eat!"

He gave her a sulking look which made her laugh. "Go into the bedroom, Moishe. I'll meet you there in ten minutes."

Inside the bedroom Morris took off his clothes and threw them, helter-skelter, on the chair. Then he got onto the old double mattress, the lumps of which he knew so well, covered himself up to his chin, and tried to make sense out of what had taken place over the last few hours.

The cracks in the ceiling of Heather's bedroom still told a story, though it was a different one each time. The jumble of lines could form themselves into a myriad of designs, depending on his mood. And the more he stared, the more they worked their way into his imagination.

Tonight they had shaped themselves into a fancy automobile. Inside it were he and Jack. Jack was looking up at the Berkeley tower from which several students had already jumped to their death that year. "I've just finished reading *Buddenbrooks*, Morris. Thanks for lending it to me. Mann could have been writing about my life, you know."

"That's why I gave it to you," Morris had replied.

"And yours too, Morris. Yours too."

Even then, Morris had laughed. Jack was a wealthy Texas scion; Morris was from the streets of New York. They were as different as blue is from red. And yet . . .

The moon was full that night, he remembered. The top of the Mercedes was down. Jack turned to him and said, "I've been offered a commission."

"A commission? To write a book?"

"No. In the Army."

"In the Army? Why would you want that, for God's sake?"

"Well, not for God's sake, Morris. More for country."

"You've got to be kidding, Jack!"

Jack shrugged. The cool smile remained on his face. "It's in the blood, Morris. Trial by fire and all that. Grandad was a general in the Confederate Army, you know."

"But Jack, you're a poet, not a soldier, damn it!"

Jack started up the Mercedes with a roar and then let the motor idle. "I was going to wait to tell you, Morris."

"When do you leave?"

"The day after tomorrow," Jack said, flicking ash from his Benson and Hedges cigarette.

A bit of glowing ember landed on Morris' trousers, quickly burning itself through. There was a painful expression on his face as he rubbed it out. "You're dangerous," Morris said.

"You injure easily," Jack replied.

Morris looked at him resentfully. "It hurt . . ."

He remembered the smile, that ghastly smile, as Jack held out one hand and, with the other, took the cigarette and ground the embers into his own palm. And he recalled the horror of the smell of burning flesh as Jack's hand began to sear.

And then the cracks disappeared into the maze.

"I'm here, Moishe."

He looked up. Heather was standing above him, nude and voluptuous, as tantalizingly desirable as the first day he had met her on the picket lines. She was smiling.

There is something, he thought to himself after it was over, about two people who've done it for a thousand times, who know every

60

nook and cranny of each other's body, what parts to touch, what parts not to touch, and when to touch them. One would think it could get awfully boring after a while. But in their case it wasn't so. It seemed to get better as the years went on.

"Nothing, no one, can harm us now," he whispered softly.

"What did you say, sweetheart?"

"I said I think I'll smoke that cigarette now."

She reached over and handed him his shirt. Feeling for the matches in her stash box, she lit one up and dangled the flame in front of him.

He took a long and grateful puff, inhaling the smoke deep into his lungs. Then he handed the cigarette over to her.

"You know I don't smoke anymore," she said. And then, taking it from his hand, she sighed, "Oh, well . . ." And she drew a puff into her lungs.

He took it back from her and put it to his lips again, savoring the taste.

"You're the only person I know who can smoke a cigarette without any guilt," said Heather with a touch of envy in her voice.

"It struck me one day," said Morris, "that people have been smoking for many years, some dying, some living on. More people smoke today than a hundred years ago, but now they have to pay a psychic tax. It's just another subliminal form of control, Heather."

She shook her head. "It's just another form of your personal death wish, Moishe."

Then she looked over at the clock on the end table and let out a groan. "Oh damn! Only four hours left before I have to get up!"

"Why don't you take the day off?" he suggested.

"That's easy for you to say, Moishe."

"Nothing's easy for me to say anymore, Heather." Looking at her seriously, he added, "Do you remember a guy named Koba?"

"Koba? How could I forget? Why do you ask, Moishe?"

"Because he called me the other day. He said he wanted to meet."

"Did you meet him?"

"We were supposed to get together yesterday at the Bohème. But he never showed." He turned to look at her face again.

"Isn't that where the old woman was shot?"

He nodded. "What do you remember about him?"

She thought for a moment. "I remember his eyes. Sometimes they were frightening. Sometimes they were lonely. Sometimes they were kind. But I didn't trust him," she said. "He was always trying to make friends with people like Kalentari from the Iranian Students' Association or Thu from the Vietnamese group. It was as if he were keeping tabs on them."

"Maybe he was," said Morris. "But maybe he was just interested in foreign events."

"Perhaps," said Heather. "But the mixture of guns and drugs and international affairs seemed to be a pretty heady brew. Stay away from him, Moishe. He's nothing but trouble."

"I met someone else, too," said Morris, his voice lowered to almost a whisper.

"Who?"

"An old friend from Berkeley."

"You mean from your undergraduate days before you went to San Francisco State? What was it, 'Old Timers' Week' yesterday?" she asked. She could tell her humor had fallen on deaf ears.

"I thought he was dead." He stared up at the ceiling and the cracks.

"Moishe?" She touched his shoulder. "Are you all right?"

He turned his face toward her. He saw her look of concern and smiled. "It wasn't a dream, Heather. He was real."

"You know, every time you begin a book you get these strange visitors. Last time it was a kangaroo."

"Yeah," he said with a wistful note in his voice. "Leon. I wonder what ever became of him?"

"Probably joined a circus or hitched a plane ride back to Australia, I suppose. But you were convinced he was real."

"Well, I needed him," said Morris somewhat defensively. "And I still think he was a good idea."

"A boxing kangaroo with a goatee and monocle as a detective's sidekick?"

"Rosa liked him."

"I rest my case."

"Characters have to come alive for me if I'm going to write about them, Heather."

"Not that alive, Moishe. You don't have to invite them for tea, for heaven's sake!"

"This one's real."

"It's just that your stupid diet is bound to give you hallucinations. Why don't you stop all this nonsense?" She closed her eyes, trying to control her frustration. "You really are impossible!"

"It wasn't a dream, Heather."

"I'm tired," she said in a sleepy voice.

The darkness had separated them again. And suddenly Morris felt a strange sensation come over his body. He touched her hand and whispered. "Heather, I'm frightened!"

But it was too late. She was fast asleep.

Chapter Five

"Jesus fucking Christ!" he shouted. "Heather! Help! I'm dying!"

"Moishe!"

"Heather! I'm dying, damn it!"

"Moishe! Stop it! You're scaring me! Heather's at work! I'm Rosa, your daughter!"

Morris opened his eyes and tried to rub out the dream. He saw her standing by the bed. Tears were streaming from her eyes. "Rosa! What's wrong? Why are you crying?"

"You frightened me, Moishe. You were yelling at the top of your lungs. You kept saying you were dying!"

"I was having a nightmare, Rosa. Haven't you ever had a nightmare?"

Rosa sat down on the edge of the bed. She wiped away her tears. "Yes — but I think I never had one like that, Moishe."

He smiled at her. "You used to come running into our bed all the time when you were a little girl. You used to say that the witches were after you."

She opened her eyes wide and stared at him. "Is that what it was? Were the witches after you?"

"No. It was the goblins."

That seemed to make sense to her. "I got over it, Moishe. You should try my technique."

"What's your technique?"

"Well, right at the part where they're just about to pounce on you, just imagine that you grow wings and fly away."

"That's a splendid idea, Rosa!" He lifted himself out of bed and took his clothes from the chair.

"I think you're the one who told it to me."

"Really?" He couldn't remember telling her that.

"I kept getting eaten by this one witch, I think her name was Maggie . . ."

"Maggie the witch! I remember her," he said as he put on his trousers.

"Well, one day, just as she was about to turn me into a chocolate chip cookie, I just sprouted wings and flew right up to the sky. Boy, she was mad as hell!"

"I don't blame her."

He went into the bathroom and splashed some water on his face.

"How come you're not in school, Rosa?" he shouted out.

"It's a holiday."

"A holiday?"

"Yep. Only for my school though." Her pixie-like face appeared at the bathroom door. "Can I come to the office with you?"

"No," he said, "I'm on an important case today."

"Honest? What's it about?"

"It's a secret. I can't tell anyone."

"Not even me?" Her mouth turned down.

"Not even you, Rosa."

"Aw, come on. I won't tell no one."

"Well, OK. I'll give you a hint. It has to do with spies, drugs and revolution."

"You gonna write a book about it, Moishe?"

"Maybe," he said, slicking back his hair with some water. Then, turning to her, he added, "I need some dough for expenses. You have anything left in your piggy bank?"

"I don't know," she said, narrowing her brow and looking at him with some suspicion. "You gonna let me hang out with you?"

He laughed. "You want to be my assistant, is that it?"

Her eyes lit up. "Yeah!"

"Well assistants have to go to school to learn how to read and write, young lady," he said, moving out of the bathroom and giving her a playful slap on the behind as he went around her on his way to the kitchen.

"I already know how to read and write, Moishe," she said,

following him. "And you told me yourself that you never learned nothing in school."

"I said 'I never learned anything in school', Rosa. But I was talking about my later years. You still have to learn the basics."

"You could teach me, Moishe," she said, sitting down across from him and watching him spread some jam on a stale piece of bread.

"Then how would I do my work if I spent my time teaching you?"

"I'd help you, that's how! You help me and I'd help you."

He went up to the stove and put the kettle on. "Well that's nice in theory, Rosa . . ."

"But in practice who wants a kid around?" she said, finishing up the sentence for him.

He fished in the cupboard for some real coffee, but only came up with the freeze-dried stuff. "What the hell does your mom drink in the morning these days?" he asked.

"Cocoa, I think."

"When I was around there used to be decent coffee on the shelves, even if I had to steal it," he said, making himself a mug of sickly-looking brew.

"Come on back home then," Rosa suggested. "We can all have coffee together."

"I will when it's my year to watch you, Rosa."

"When's that, Moishe?"

He sat back down at the table and drank. "Ask your mom."

"I see you're off your diet," she said pointing to the bread and jam.

He looked at the food as if he hadn't noticed it before. "Yeah, every so often . . ." Then he winked, "Don't tell Heather, though."

She made a face. "So you want a loan?" she asked him.

"How much you got?" he replied, gulping down the coffee.

"Seven bucks."

"How much interest you charge these days?"

"For you, nothing."

He got up and tucked in his shirt. "What's the catch, Rosa?"

She got up too. "No catch. Just let me spend the day with you."

66

"What about school?"

"What about it?"

"Well you can't just cut school forever, Rosa. Besides, Heather would find out."

"No she won't."

He walked back to the bedroom to get his jacket. "Yes she will. The principal will call her."

Through the open door he could hear the telephone being dialed. He walked back into the hallway. Rosa was on the phone. She put up a finger for him to wait.

"Hello? Is this the principal's office? I'm sorry to be calling you so late but my daughter, Rosa Kaplan, has a dentist appointment today and she won't be coming to school. She's in Mrs Smith's class. Yes, all day. She's having five fillings. Yes, she eats way too much sugar. Certainly, I'll have her bring a note tomorrow. Thank you."

Rosa hung up the telephone and smiled. "Ta da!" she sang, extending her arms like Shirley Temple at the end of a song-and-dance routine.

He shook his head. "You little sneak!" He tried to say it in a reprimanding way, but he couldn't help a tiny smile.

"So what ya say, Moishe? Do I get the job or not?"

"You'll need a cap," he said, before he even realized he had relented.

"Why's that?"

"Because every good investigator has a cap. It's part of the act."

She went into the hall closet and pulled down a box. "Heather keeps some old stuff in here," she said. "I thought I saw a blue cap one day. Yeah. Here it is!" She pulled it out and put it on her head. "How do I look, Moishe?"

He laughed. "Just like one of the *Dead End* kids. You got the expense money?"

She patted her pocket. "Right in here."

"OK, let's go then."

"Hey," she said, stopping at the door. "What about your cap?"

He reached inside his jacket pocket, got out his leather cap and put it on. "How do I look?" he asked her.

"Great!" she said. "I like that flower in your lapel too. Where'd you get it Moishe?"

"You like it?" he said taking it off and sticking it into the buttonhole of her jacket. "It's yours!" Then, grabbing her hand, he pulled her out, shutting the door behind them.

"Any messages for me?" Morris asked Larry, the counter man, as he and Rosa sauntered into the Meat Market Café. It was mid-morning and the place was starting to fill with shaky caffeine addicts.

Larry ran his fingers through his long, Rasputin-like beard and said, "It seems to me you did get a call, Morris." He rummaged through some papers by the cash register. "Ah, here it is. It's from the Virgin Mary." Handing the note to him and narrowing his eyes, he said, "I didn't know you had anything to do with that, Morris."

Morris took the folded paper and read it. "Meeting tonight of the Mother Joneses in memory of a fallen comrade. At the Farm. Eight o'clock. Pot Luck. Bring a vegetable. Be there, Morris! TVM."

"Hey, Moishe! Can I come too?" asked Rosa, standing on her tiptoes so she could sneak a look.

"Where?"

"To your meeting. What's a 'fallen comrade'?"

"A euphemism, Rosa, for a stinker who expired."

"Can I come?"

"No. It's not for kids. Besides, Heather's looking after you tonight."

"What if Heather says I can come?"

"She'll say 'no'. What do you want to drink?"

"Same thing you're having, boss."

Morris grimaced. "All right, Rosa. Cut the banter. Give me two bucks from the expense account and then go find a seat in the office."

"Right, boss!" she said throwing him a salute. She reached into her pocket and brought out two crumpled dollar bills. Then she skipped off to the former refrigeration-room.

"New recruit?" asked Larry, pumping out a double espresso on the machine.

"Yeah, I'm thinking of sending her on her first suicide mission today. You got the card ready for me yet?"

"Not yet, Morris, but I'm working on it." Larry was an expert cartoonist in the style of R Cobb who would loved to have done the early "blood and guts" comics that were banned in the '50s by overzealous parent committees. Morris had assigned him to do his calling card: "Morris Kaplan, Investigator. Meat Market Café, San Francisco. No Job Too Big Or Small. (No Divorces.)"

Larry's first idea was to have a full-figure cartoon of Morris, pen in one hand, staring through a magnifying glass at an enormous fingerprint below, while a giant, hairy paw hovering overhead, was about to crush him. Morris had said that somehow it didn't seem to be the statement he really wanted to make. However, since Morris had paid nothing on account, Larry, sensibly, had put the project at the end of his list — right after a sign for the local Cub Scout New Year's marshmallow roast (a *tour de force*, months in the planning, that was to have salivating wolves lurking behind the bushes and several ghouls stationed inconspicuously among the cubbies, roasting arms and legs on their twigs instead of fluffy candy).

"What's the kid having today?" asked Larry, handing Morris his cup of espresso.

"Warm milk," Morris replied.

"Anything in it?"

"Arsenic if you've got it."

"Really, Morris?" said Larry in a low voice that seemed to quiver a bit.

"Just give me the milk, Larry."

Rosa's face dropped when she saw Morris bringing the drinks back. "What's that stuff?" she asked.

"Milk. Drink up."

"What's in your cup?"

"Coffee."

"Wanna trade?"

"No."

Suddenly her expression changed. There was a look of fear in her eyes. "Moishe, there's a guy who looks just like that awful picture you drew yesterday."

Morris turned quickly, his heart racing. "Koba?" Then seeing no one, he whispered, "Where is he, Rosa?"

Rosa shrugged and sipped her coffee. Morris looked down and saw the glass of warm milk in front of him.

"Fun and games, huh?" said Morris, switching the glasses again.

"Yech!" Rosa made a face. "What is that stuff?"

"It's something that grows hair on the palms of your hands, Rosa. But if you want, I'll mix a little into your milk." He put two teaspoonfuls of espresso into her glass. "A bit of espresso in your milk and it's called a *caffelatte*."

Rosa tasted it, hesitantly. Then she smiled. "I like!" she exclaimed as the mixture settled on her palate.

"Good," said Morris. And, looking at her sternly, he said, "No more tricks!"

"OK, boss. Let's get down to work."

Morris stared at her for a moment, shook his head and sighed. Taking a pen and paper from his pocket, he began to write.

"What's that?" asked Rosa, leaning forward, her curiosity aroused.

"It's a casebook," said Morris.

"You mean you're really investigating an honest-to-goodness case? Wow! What case is that, Moishe?"

He put down his pen in exasperation and looked at her. She was staring back at him with wide, innocent eyes. "OK," he said. "There's been a murder. Right?"

"Right! Uh, who's been murdered, Moishe? The comrade guy in the note that no one liked? How come no one liked him, Moishe?"

"Because he was a putz, Rosa. So let that be a lesson to you. Don't be a putz."

"What's the putz's name, Moishe?"

"Philip. The putz was named Philip. And he was killed. Shot at his front door."

"Who shot him?"

"I don't know."

She looked at him with a puzzled face. "Moishe, there's one thing I don't understand."

"What's that?"

"If no one liked him — this Philip guy — why are you spending so much time trying to find out who done it?"

"I'm not spending 'so much time', Rosa. In fact, I haven't even started yet. But it is a good question and the answer is . . ."

"Yeah?"

"Well, even though he was a putz he was still on our side. At least I think he was on our side . . ." He stopped for a second. "How much expense money do we have left?"

"Five bucks," she replied.

"Well, hand it over. I need some cigarettes."

"Are you gonna let me solve the case with you?"

"No."

"Why not?"

"Because this is serious stuff and I don't want you to get hurt."

"What's serious stuff? A putz gets bumped off. You don't know who done it and no one cares. What's so dangerous?"

"Because there's more to it, Rosa. Someone else is hanging around who knew us back then and who may have had something to do with Philip's murder. If he did, then we're all in danger."

"Even me?"

"No. Not you. You don't have anything to be afraid of."

"Why do you think he's after you, Moishe? You got any evidence?"

"I'm working on instinct right now. That's how all good investigators work — on instinct. Facts come later."

"I don't understand. What's this instinct business?"

"Instinct is when you think something is going on but you're not quite sure why it's happening."

"But you got to have more to go on than that, Moishe. I mean, I've seen detective films. You got to have clues."

"Well I do have clues. And I was about to put them down in the casebook before you started getting all smarty with me."

She made a pouting expression with her lips.

"OK," he said pushing the paper and pencil to her side. "If you really want to be my assistant, you can get busy."

"Doing what?"

"Writing. You can write can't you?"

"Yeah, I can write," she said. "What do you want me to put down?"

"Label one page 'What We Know'."

She scrawled the words where he had indicated and then looked back up at him. "What next, Moishe?"

"Now make a '1' and write 'Putz killed'. OK. Label another page 'What We Don't Know', put another '1' and write 'By whom'."

"Gottcha."

"Back to 'What We Know'. Under '2' write 'Koba reappears'."

"Koba's with a 'K'? That's the guy you're scared of, right?"

"Right. But under 'What We Don't Know, 2' you better write 'If Koba did it'."

Rosa studied the list. "It doesn't look like we're getting very far, Moishe."

"Well, it's just the beginning, Rosa. You can't expect to solve the case in the first five minutes."

"Don't we have any other clues?"

"A couple. We know Koba's lawyer when he was busted in '69. His name's Rocky Calhoon. He's the same guy who defended me and Heather."

"So he goes under 'What We Know, Number 3'."

"And we know the cop who's in charge of the case. Brian Murphy, SFPD."

"'What We Know, Number 4'."

"But what we don't know, '3', is whether Rocky Calhoon can help us or, '4', whether Murphy will talk to us."

"Why wouldn't he talk to us, Moishe? We're citizens, ain't we?"

"As far as Murphy's concerned, that's probably debatable. He thought we should have all been shipped back to Russia."

"I thought you were born in New York?"

"I was. But Murphy thinks Brooklyn is just another name for the USSR."

"Any other clues?"

"Make a heading on another page. Title it 'Strange Events'. Put under '1', 'Old woman shot outside café where I was going to meet Koba'."

She looked at him oddly. "I don't get it. Why were you going to meet Koba? I thought you were scared of him. And who's the old lady who got shot?"

"I went to meet Koba because he asked me to meet him and I wanted to hear what he had to say. I don't know who the old lady was who got shot. All I know is that the bullet wasn't meant for her . . ."

She looked up at him again. "Who was the bullet meant for, Moishe?"

He felt the words stick in his throat. "I don't know."

"Do I list that too?"

"Why not?" He let out a sigh.

"Anything else under 'Strange Events'?"

"Put down: 'Accosted by college friend I thought was dead. Wanted me to help him write a story'."

"No kidding?" said Rosa, much impressed. "Does he have a publisher in mind?"

"I wouldn't doubt it. He wasn't the sort to jump into things without having everything set up in advance . . ."

She saw that he seemed to be drifting away. "Something wrong, Moishe?"

"No," said Morris, rubbing his chin. "I was just thinking."

"So what do we do now?"

Morris got up from the table. "We take the casebook over to Fredo and let him examine it."

"Oh, good!" said Rosa, who loved to go visiting. "Do you think he'll let me watch TV?"

"What is this?" Fredo asked, looking down at the notations which had been thrust into his hand after he had answered their persistent shouts and led them, reluctantly, inside his cave.

"It's the casebook," said Rosa.

73

"Casebook?" Fredo looked at Morris questioningly. Morris shrugged his shoulders in response.

Rosa did a quick inspection of the room and ended up by Fredo's desk. "Hey, Fredo," she called. "What's all these drawings? You gonna be a cartoonist like Larry?"

"It's a project," said Fredo in a ruffled sort of way. He walked over and folded the papers, slipping them back into a file. "You should ask before you start looking at things," he reprimanded.

"Can I watch TV?" she said with a forced politeness.

"Yeah," said Fredo. "If I can find it."

Morris chuckled. "How can you lose a TV?"

Fredo started moving stacks of newspapers from one table to another. "I could lose an elephant in here, Morris."

Meanwhile, Rosa had discovered the mouse. "He's a cutie, Fredo!" she said, as the mouse tried to nibble her extended finger through the glass. "What's his name? How come you're keeping him in a fish bowl filled with grass?"

Fredo looked over at the frisky rodent and made a dour expression. "His name is Shithead." Then glancing at Morris he said, "He's eating me out of house and home. I bet he's devoured three pounds of that mold already. All he does is eat it and shit it out. He loves the stuff."

"Aw," said Rosa, already deeply in love, "he's adorable!"

"You can have him if you want," said Fredo who had finally discovered the TV under a pile of unwashed shirts. "I'm finished with the little creep."

"Really? I can? Wow, thanks Fredo!"

"That's OK," he said. "It's either you or the neighborhood cat. What do you want to watch?" he asked her, turning from one channel to another.

"The Million Dollar Movie. It's on Channel 2. You got any popcorn?"

"No. I got a beer though. You want a beer?"

"Sure," she said, already engrossed in the flickering images.

"Can she have a beer?" Fredo asked Morris. "I mean, I don't know much about kids. Is it OK?"

"Give her some juice and tell her it's beer. She'll never know the difference."

"I don't have juice."

"Give her some water." As an afterthought he said, "And put in a few spoons of that mold."

"No, I couldn't do that," Fredo said, filling up a cloudy glass at the sink. "She might barf on the floor."

While Fredo took the glass to Rosa, who was now nearly comatose from the effects of the alpha waves, Morris watched the goings-on in the rear garden through the window above the kitchen sink.

"Is that the chiropractor?" asked Morris, pointing outside.

"Yeah," said Fredo, gritting his teeth. "Just look at them cavorting around like that."

Morris was looking. There were four of them, the chiropractor and three young, buxom women, splashing around in the hot tub.

"He does this every day?" asked Morris with some amazement.

"It's part of his so-called therapy," Fredo said with a belch. "But not for long. Not for long . . ."

"What a moralist you are!" Morris said. "How did you ever get through the '60s? You lived in the Haight, Fredo."

"This is different, Morris. This is *la dolce vita*, the decadence of the bourgeoisie. I don't mind young kids screwing in the park — that's just puppy lust. But this! This is truly disgusting!"

"I've seen worse things in the fur department of I Magnin," said Morris.

"Imagine having a creep like that messing with your backbone!" said Fredo in the tone of someone who had just seen a botched appendectomy.

"I admit that I would have my reservations," said Morris, who didn't let anyone, with the exception of Heather, mess with his backbone.

"Besides, he's trying to evict me."

"He wants to evict you? Well join the crowd. It seems we're all being evicted from this city in one way or another. What's his excuse?"

"He wants to turn the basement into a wine cellar."

"A wine cellar?"

"Yeah. And a storehouse for his randy meats."

"Randy meats?"

75

"Do you know how few natural resources there are left to share with five billion people? He's probably squandered more than the total allocation of two thousand Chinese peasants."

"In his hot tub?"

"You should see his barbecues, Morris. Hams, turkeys, filleted steaks, potatoes floating in great seas of butter — it's obscene!"

"I can imagine. That water must get pretty messy after a while."

"I sometimes dream of him choking on a turkey leg while he's screwing one of his patients in the Jacuzzi."

Morris shook his head in wonder. "Fredo, can I use your telephone?"

"Sure, Morris. It's someplace around here," he said, looking about. "I used it yesterday."

"I want to try and get in touch with Rocky Calhoon."

Fredo stopped his search and stared at him. "You're really serious about this, aren't you?"

"Of course, Fredo!"

"Some things should just be allowed to rest, Morris. Like random bullets through open doors," Fredo said, pulling nervously on his moustache.

"But you're the one who said that there was no such thing as an accidental shooting," Morris reminded him.

"That's true. On the other hand, you can't bring back the dead."

Morris thought of his strange meeting with Jack Chesterton last night and furrowed his brow. "But you might be able to prevent a replay," he muttered.

"You can also cause a replay," said Fredo, narrowing his eyes.

"You can only die once."

Fredo made a movement of resignation with his hands. "Have it your own way," he said. "But don't say I didn't warn you if you end up with a bullet in your head."

"OK," said Morris. "It's a promise. Where's your phone?"

Fredo had found the cord and was following it through its twists and turns around the room. It led eventually to the refrigerator. "Oh, yeah," he said, opening the icebox door, "I put it here last night so I could work undisturbed."

"Must have been an important project," said Morris, taking the chilled receiver in his hands.

"It has possibilities," said Fredo.

Morris got Rocky Calhoon's number from information and then dialed the appropriate digits with his arthritic index finger. A secretarial voice answered on the second ring: "Mr Calhoon's office. Who's speaking please?"

"This is Morris Kaplan. Is Rocky there?"

"Is that 'Kaplan' with a 'K' or a 'C'? she asked.

"Will the answer to that question determine whether he's in or not?"

"I beg your pardon?"

"It's with a 'K'," Morris said.

"Just a moment. I'll see whether he's in."

Morris was wondering whether it was possible that Rocky could have sneaked past her desk, like a thief in the night, without her knowing it, when Rocky's exuberant voice came on the line: "Morris! How the hell are you! Not busted again, I hope!"

"Not since '69," said Morris. "How's tricks, Rocky?"

"Can't complain. Not as exciting as the old days, Morris. But, as they say, you can't have love and money, too."

"Who says that, Rocky?"

"What, Morris?"

"Listen, Rocky, I need to talk with you about a case I'm working on."

"You in the practice now, Morris?"

"So to speak. But I don't do divorces."

"Too bad. That's where the money is."

"Yeah. Well this is kind of urgent. You think we could have a few words today?"

"Today? I'm kind of busy . . ."

"I'd really appreciate it, Rocky. Maybe I could just squeeze a couple of minutes out of you."

"All right. Come over around noon. Clara's out to lunch then, so just walk right in."

"Sure thing. Thanks Rocky." Hanging up, he looked at Fredo, who was watching him in amazement, and said, "You want it back in the fridge?"

Fredo shook his head. "You're nuts!" he said.

"By the way," Morris said, getting ready to leave, "did Mary call you about the wake tonight?"

"That's why the phone was in the fridge," Fredo replied.

"Well, I'll see you there."

"Not likely. I wouldn't waste my time."

Morris shrugged and started out the door.

"Haven't you forgotten something?" he asked, pointing back at Rosa.

"Oh, yeah," said Morris. "Is it OK if the kid stays with you? Tell her I had to meet my lawyer. She understands things like that."

"What am I supposed to do with her?" asked Fredo, looking a little panicked.

"She'll sit there like a rock till the film is over. Then send her and the mouse back to Heather. She knows her way home," he said as he hurried out the door.

Chapter Six

Rocky Calhoon was old-line San Francisco left. His rough-and-tumble immigrant Irish father had made good in the legal trade, due partly to a fortuitous marriage which gave him the necessary "blue blood" connections, and partly to a razor tongue and trenchant wit which quickly gained a following within the labor movement of the day.

The son was not quite a chip off the old block, looking more like a model for Arrow shirts than a bar-room bruiser. But he had won his spurs during the Great San Francisco State College Strike of 1968, defending the radicals for the various felonies and misdemeanors that had been thrown at them by a vindictive administration. And, because of that, his head bore the scars of several late-night truncheon blows when the boys in blue decided to show him who was really boss. In the end it was his father who defended him, much to the dismay of Brian Murphy, another son of an immigrant Irishman, whose troops had led the charge that fateful night.

Rocky's feet were on a great mahogany desk, balanced atop the "out" tray when Morris arrived. He was eating a banana.

"Morris!" Rocky called out, grinning from ear to ear and unwrapping himself to stand up. "I was just thinking about the time you were being dragged down the hall at city jail on the way to the prison barber and screaming for me to get you an injunction."

"How come you didn't?" asked Morris, shaking Rocky's extended hand.

"I tried," said Rocky. "I really did. But I had a murder case that took precedence."

"Over severed follicles? You always had a strange set of priorities, Rocky."

"Sit down, Morris," Rocky laughed. "Tell me what's been going on with the revolution while I've been keeping the dope peddlers out of the clink." As he spoke he opened up the hat drawer of his desk, exposing what looked like a bale of hay.

"I haven't seen anything like that since the Mendocino marijuana harvest of '73!" Morris focused his eyes on the enormous stash.

"Well, it pays to have important clients," said Rocky, pulling a few buds from the bundle and then rolling them into a smoke. He lit up and passed the joint to Morris.

Morris took a courtesy puff despite his pledge of abstinence, and said, "That's what I wanted to talk with you about, Rocky — one of your clients."

"You mean Roger?"

"Roger? What's he done?"

"Who are we talking about, Morris?" Rocky was starting to look confused.

"Koba. I wanted to ask you about Koba."

Rocky drew in a quick hiss of smoke. "Now that takes me back a long way," he said. "What a character!"

"Did you know him very well?" asked Morris, taking another drag out of politeness as Rocky passed the smouldering roach his way.

"No, can't say as I did. He was a hard one to know. Very taciturn, but very intense."

"Who busted him?" asked Morris, handing back the roach.

"Murphy. Who else? Probably the one time in his life he actually nabbed the right man."

"What do you mean, Rocky?"

"Well, I can't begin to tell you all the phony charges of assault and battery I defended, or all the magic drug busts . . ."

"Magic drug busts?"

"Yeah, now you see it, now you don't." He smiled. "Don't act so innocent, Morris. Didn't they once try to stick you with punching a fuzz?"

"I wish I did punch him," said Morris. "At least I would have gotten some pleasure out of it then."

"Nine times out of ten, people are punished for what they

80

didn't do, not for what they did. So you might as well go ahead and do it, if you want to."

"And Koba wanted to, all right."

"And he did it."

"Do you think he was for real, Rocky?" The room had begun to spin as the drug entered his bloodstream.

"Well, yes and no. I think he was sincere, but like all the crazies there was a thin line between him and the cops. He wanted a revolution — any shape, any kind — and he was willing to do anything to get it started. When you take that attitude, Morris, you're bound for trouble. You start making some pretty strange alliances."

"He was busted for selling guns to the Black Defense League, wasn't he?"

"Among other things. And as we know, half those guys were in the FBI."

"So was he an agent or not?"

Rocky shrugged. "I don't have any evidence, Morris. But why the sudden interest in him anyway?"

"You know about Philip Lampam?"

"Yeah. Tragic." Rocky seemed to be studying Morris' face. "What's that got to do with Koba?"

"Maybe nothing. But I got a call from Koba just the other day. He's back in town."

Suddenly Rocky's body tensed. He got up from his chair and went to the window which overlooked Dolores Park. He opened it and gazed outside. "That's very strange," he said.

"I thought so too," said Morris.

Rocky turned back toward him. "It's very strange, Morris, because Koba is dead."

"What do you mean?" Morris stood up and felt the ground start to wobble under his feet.

"Whoever phoned you must have been pretending to be Koba."

"But how do you know he's dead, Rocky? I thought he skipped bail and vanished from sight!"

"That's how I know. Flight to avoid prosecution is a Federal offense. As Koba's defense attorney, I was informed when the body was discovered."

"Where was it discovered?"

"In Bolivia. Seems like Koba had gotten involved with the guerrillas there. He was killed by the Bolivian army. He's dead, Morris. Whoever called you was an impostor."

By the time Morris had left Rocky's office, the walls were getting wavy and the floor was like a sandy beach at riptide. He made his perilous way across the street and staggered into the corner store.

"Where're your chocolate chip cookies?" he asked the kid behind the counter.

"What kind do you want?" said the young man. "We have seventeen different brands."

"It doesn't matter," said Morris. "Just let me have a pack."

"It would help if you told me what you're smoking," said the grocer. "'Uncle Andy's', for example, is good with Panama Red. I suggest 'Mother's' if you're puffing Acapulco Gold."

"This stuff is more like Martian Purple."

"Well then I don't know. Maybe Nabisco."

He took the cookies to Dolores Park and tore the package open, stuffing several in his mouth at once. A young woman, walking with her child, glanced at him suspiciously.

"Look!" shouted the little boy excitedly to his mother. "That man's eating all those by himself!"

The woman quickened her pace. Morris couldn't hear her emphatic whispers, but he suspected it had something to do with ignoring strangers stuffing themselves with cookies in the park.

As he waited for the sugar to counteract the drainage from his brain, he thought of the irony — sitting at the very place where he had waited so many years ago after pleading with Rocky to help get Heather out of jail.

"You know the only reason they stuck her with that sentence is that she's a radical," he had told him.

"Yeah," said Rocky, "but it's only thirty days, Morris. She'll be out by Christmas."

"Thirty days in jail for attending a rally seems pretty stiff."

"They could have charged her with assault, Morris. That would have been a felony."

82

"They could have charged her with murder, Rocky. Then they could have given her the chair."

He thought about when he had visited her at the "Women's Facility", a euphemism which reminded him of "Outhouse", up in the San Bruno hills. The day before the earth had shaken, striking 4.3 on the Richter scale. And he dreamed she had fallen into a vast chasm that had opened up under her cell, without a chance to say "goodbye".

Her hair fell softly over her eyes the day he came to see her. She was dressed in prison grey. Like an unbleached muslin sack, it hid her figure inside its starched surroundings. To him, she looked for all the world like an imprisoned deer. Her large fawn eyes covered by a hint of mistiness. Her fragile skin seeped in disinfectant.

The matron stared at them like a latter-day Madame Lafarge, waiting patiently for the guillotine to fall. And when he left, he felt the sadness of a precious soul in bondage. Thirty years, thirty days, thirty hours. His heart ached nonetheless.

Rocky got her out in twenty and he thanked him much for that. But there were scars. Even twenty days in prison leaves its mark. He saw it in her eyes and in the way she moved. He saw it as a loss of innocence.

Heather told him of the other women there, the ones she never would have met except in jail. They were the castaways, the whores, the addicts, the petty thieves. She told him of the woman who cried all night for the baby lost inside her, screaming till the matron came and hosed her down. She told him of the woman who had ripped her mattress into shreds and stuffed it down the loo because she couldn't stand the loneliness, the isolation, the inhumanity. And she told him of the whore who said, "Listen, honey, don't trust a man on smack 'cause he'll always do you wrong." They were all caged together in that unholy zoo. And they had come to know each other's pain.

There was something peculiar, he thought, when he reached the garden path which led to his cottage. Arnold was always meticulous about closing the gate but now it stood open.

There was another feeling, too, as he climbed the rickety stairs

— nothing he could easily define, just an aura. And he felt his stomach muscles tighten as he reached inside his pocket for his keys and realized they weren't there.

He tried the door. It opened.

"Hello, Morris," a voice said clearly.

He heard the voice before he saw the face. As his eyes adjusted to the pale light, he made out a figure sitting at his table, drinking from his special fifth of whisky. It was Jack.

"I hope you don't mind," he said. "I found your keys on the steps and I let myself in." He was still wearing his coat and hat, but somehow he seemed quite at home in Morris' chair.

"Make yourself comfortable. Have some whisky," said Morris, still somewhat startled and not knowing whether to be annoyed at the intrusion or happy to see his old friend again.

Jack held up his glass. "I already have. I found it in the cabinet. You don't mind?" He said it in a tone which smacked of *noblesse oblige*.

"I was saving it for a special occasion," said Morris, pouring himself a drink and then pulling up a chair, "but I suppose this qualifies."

"To old times," said Jack, winking as he put the glass to his lips.

Morris studied his face and wondered what strange events had made their mark so deep that furrows were now etched where once there had been none. Recalling that his own face was mapped too, he repeated, "To old times and new mysteries — of which, Jack, you are one."

Jack laughed. "I know it's a bit melodramatic and all that. But believe me, it's the only way . . ."

"For what?" asked Morris.

"To meet you — unobserved."

Morris rubbed his eyes. "I think you're about fifteen years too late, Jack," he said. "There's not much purpose in them observing me anymore."

"It's not you I'm talking about, Morris."

"OK," said Morris, staring at his old friend, now a stranger. "What's up? How come you tracked me down after all these years? What kind of trouble are you in?"

84

Jack took another swallow of whisky and said, "There's something you should know, Morris. I didn't go to Vietnam . . ."

"You said that last night. I thought the Army sent everyone to Vietnam back then."

"I wasn't in the Army."

"You weren't?" Morris looked at him curiously.

"No. It was a different branch. A different service."

"I don't understand, Jack. What are you saying?"

"I joined the firm," he said, taking another drink and then looking deeply into Morris' eyes.

"The firm? What firm?"

"I joined the Company, Morris. Do you understand me now?"

Suddenly it registered. Morris felt a vein in his forehead start to bulge. "Jack! Are you saying that while I was fighting for the revolution, you were in the CIA?"

Jack smiled. "See what curiosities twenty odd years can hold?"

Morris shook his head like an aggrieved rabbi and looked down into his glass. "Jack, how could you? I mean, I'd forgive anything — almost. You could have been a gangster or even a heroin salesman and I could have forgiven you. But the CIA?"

"And what of you, Morris? Have you led a life of pristine innocence for all these years?"

Morris looked up at his strange accuser. "Me? What have I done?"

"Well, we can start with your wife and child."

"What do you know about them?" Morris glared at him.

"Remember who I worked for. I had access to your file, Morris. I know a great deal."

He ran his fingers through his hair and shaking his head back and forth, he muttered, "I can't believe it. I can't believe you're sitting here telling me you were in the fucking CIA and you read my fucking file and you know about my fucking wife and child!"

"I know a lot more than that," said Jack, taking another drink of Morris' special whisky.

Morris looked up at him challengingly. "You know where I was on June 18, 1969?"

"You were in prison with the rest of the kids who got tired of cops and robbers and decided to play revolutionary."

"And where were you, smug asshole?" Morris said between his teeth.

Jack looked at him without saying anything and then downed what was left of his drink. Finally he muttered, "In South America, making the world safe for General Motors." Then, lifting the bottle, he said, "Mind if I have another?"

"Go ahead. I'm surprised you even asked. You guys usually take what you want anyway. I'm not going to deny liquor to someone with a license to kill, am I?"

Jack filled up his glass to the brim and poured a like amount into Morris'. "You know," he said, "there's a crucial point you're missing."

"I think I get the point well enough," said Morris, trying to drown the bitter taste in his mouth by filling it with alcohol.

"What you're missing, Morris, is that I've left. I've come in from the cold. I'm on your side now, old boy."

There was a mean smirk on Morris' lips. "You're saying you want to confess your crimes? Is that it?"

"Well, Morris, you're not far wrong. In fact, that's exactly what I'd like to do. But I need your help."

"Why my help, Jack? All you need is a pencil and paper and then a sword to fall on."

"The sword might come later, Morris. And it might not be of my hand. I need your help because, at the moment, my life's not worth a plugged nickel. I need someone I can trust to get my story out, if . . ."

"If you finally get what you deserve?"

Jack smiled disarmingly. "Bluntness was always your best quality, Morris. That's why I liked you. There weren't too many people back then who spoke their mind."

"Maybe your problem was you didn't listen when they did."

"Perhaps, but that's whisky under the bridge, wouldn't you say?"

Morris took his glass and drank. To his own surprise, his abhorrence was being slowly overcome by curiosity. He suddenly felt a need to know how Jack, a former friend, had been transformed into something that, in his mind, was very much akin to a werewolf.

86

"How the hell were you recruited into the CIA?"

"Through contacts. My dad was in oil, you remember. He knew a lot of that sort. It's a network, Morris. If you come from the right family, know the right people, go to the right school, you're approached."

"But what made you decide to go? It's one thing to be approached by the devil; it's quite another to sell your soul . . ."

Jack smiled, perhaps a bit condescendingly Morris thought. "I was a rich kid. I had a romantic view of life. I knew I'd have to do national service and the idea of doing that blindly didn't appeal to me."

"You could have gotten a deferment like the rest of us."

"I didn't want a deferment. It was an obligation that I wanted to fulfill. Besides, the life of a spy seemed a lot more glamorous than that of a graduate student — or so I thought."

Morris gritted his teeth.

"You have to look at this in the context of the time," Jack continued. "Krushchev was pounding his shoe on the table at the UN saying he'd bury us. I believed him."

"You were a poet, Jack . . ."

"Poetry is for children," he said, lighting up a cigarette. "I wanted to be a man. I wanted to have a career." He let the smoke drift from his mouth as he pondered something in his mind. "But the Company doesn't offer you a job like IBM. They're far more devious. They snare you like a miserable donkey who thinks he's a stallion. They make you feel like they can't run the agency without you and then, just as their seduction is complete, they pull the rug out from under."

"How do you mean?"

"As soon as you start thinking how appealing it would be to have a secret identity and take your fantasy games into the world of adults — just at that moment they turn the tables on you and make it seem doubtful that you'll ever qualify."

"Hadn't they vetted you already?"

"They wanted you to build up a psychological dependence on them, Morris. They wanted you to believe they had something over you. And if there was nothing, then something had to be invented."

"Future blackmail, huh?"

"Exactly. And then there was the barrage of pledges: 'I shall never under any circumstances divulge . . .'; 'Under threat of prosecution, I promise . . .' It was endless. But we signed everything and anything for the privilege of becoming a spy for God and Country." Jack crushed out his cigarette in a little dish sitting on the table.

He lit up another smoke and continued. "The polygraph became our parish priest. Throughout our career we always had our periodic sessions. It was our place of ultimate accountability — our moments of truth. We couldn't trust our friends or lovers, only the polygraph machine."

"Ah, brave new world," sighed Morris, sipping at his whisky. In fact, he was becoming more fascinated as Jack went on. "So where were you assigned?"

"Peru. My job there was pretty far removed from cloak-and-dagger stuff. It was very routine work. No imagination was needed. I was in charge of photocopying the mail sent to Cuba, Russia, East Germany, Poland, and any other nation that supposedly flew the red flag. Every single letter with that stated destination passed through my hand so every one was photocopied. You have no idea, Morris, how many tedious hours I spent steaming them open and gluing them shut."

"And the Peruvian government allowed it?"

"Allowed it? Morris, they were happy for our services! After a year I was transferred to Uruguay. It was there I learned to fight the good fight against communist subversion. I learned how to use trusted go-betweens to pay out money for sources within the government, the opposition parties, the police, the Left. In fact, within a very short time my access to information became so good that I was often able to obtain transcripts of the cabinet meetings before the cabinet ministers themselves received them," said Jack with a note of pride.

"You bugged the cabinet chambers?" asked Morris.

"No. It was simply a matter of paying a small stipend to the clerk who typed them up. But what was truly satisfying was running black documents by the press. It's something like a forger seeing his art for sale at Christie's. Can you imagine a prestigious newspaper publishing a story on its front page that you had just concocted the night before? Think about it, Morris!"

Morris was thinking about it. "Just another weapon in the arsenal of your destabilization program, I suspect."

"You're right. It was only one of a hundred different tools. When you have access to privileged information, when you control central computers that generate the data and statistics, the very pulse of an economy, it isn't difficult to chart a scientific course of action against any party, any group, or any government we wish to weaken or remove."

"And you did weaken and remove. Just you and your tiny staff?"

"With the help of the greedy, Morris. Always with the help of the greedy."

"So when did you get fed up?"

Jack tried to squeeze a few more drops out of the whisky bottle. "It didn't happen all at once. You see, whatever you might think, I accepted the argument that, in the end, my job could be justified by progress — that poverty would slowly disappear, that justice, American justice, would eventually prevail. And if certain liberties had to be curtailed in pursuit of genuine freedom of enterprise, where everyone could aspire to greatness, no matter what their class or background, it was just the price to be paid for the greater good."

Morris cringed. "You could run for President on that speech, Jack."

"But then I began to wonder whether the game was a farce." Jack shook his head. He seemed weary. "After all those years of subterfuge and betrayal, things only seemed to be getting worse. And one day it struck me that there was never a hope that poverty would be eradicated, because it was that very poverty which gave the Company its power. For the Company's only claim to loyalty, its only access to information, to spies, to henchmen, to traitors, lay simply in the fact that it could offer better wages — it could outbid all competitors."

For the first time that evening, Morris began to feel a trace of sympathy for his old friend. His words had sincerely moved him.

And he watched closely as Jack lit up another cigarette and continued with his thoughts.

"Soon I began to view myself as a pimp for American corporations, helping to squeeze natural resources from the lands like slaughtered pigs being drained of their last drops of blood, while all around children were dying of curable diseases and mothers were selling their daughters to fat businessmen for the price of a loaf of bread."

Jack tried to pour himself another drink. "The bottle's empty," he said.

"But there must have been something that happened, Jack. Something that pushed you over the brink. I mean a lot of CIA guys must get disillusioned. But they don't leave . . ."

"There was," said Jack. He stood up. "It's a long story though. Maybe we can continue it tomorrow."

The whisky bottle lay on its side. Morris felt his head throb. He didn't expect what he said next. The words just came out of his mouth.

"Jack, before you go — there's something I want to ask . . ."

Jack stood by the door. "What is it Morris?"

"There's a guy named Koba who was around in '68. Later he went to South America and got involved with the Bolivian guerrillas. I understand he was killed over there."

The light was dim by the door. Morris could hardly make out Jack's face. "What did you want to know?"

"Someone phoned me the other day claiming to be Koba."

"Maybe Koba isn't dead after all, Morris."

"What do you mean?" Morris felt his body grow cold.

"I still have a few contacts. I'll try to find out what I can for you."

"Thanks," said Morris. "I'd appreciate it."

Jack opened up the door. It was almost dark outside. "I think it would be better if you didn't tell anyone I was around."

"I understand," said Morris.

The door remained open. He watched Jack disappear like a ghost into the evening mist.

Chapter Seven

He heard her voice say, "You call this being 'on the wagon', Moishe?"

Opening his eyes, he saw Heather standing before him with her arms crossed.

"Did you finish that all by yourself?"

"What?" he asked innocently.

"That bottle of whisky," she said, pointing her finger at the evidence.

"No. I had a friend."

"Well, never mind," she sighed. "Maybe you want to wash up —or are you going *au naturel*, as they say on the Barbary Coast."

"Are we going someplace?" He looked at her uncomprehendingly.

"The wake, as you so nicely put it, Morris, is this evening. I know you had a special invitation."

He groaned. "Oh, that!"

"Yes, 'that'," she replied, somewhat sarcastically.

"Heather," he said, rubbing his bleary eyes. "I'm onto an important investigation . . ."

"Button up your shirt," she said, opening the door. "Fame can wait another few hours."

The top was down on Heather's ancient English Ford. Morris, however, didn't see Rosa slumped in the back until he slid across the seat and turned around.

"What's she doing here?" asked Morris, poking his thumb toward the rear.

Heather started up the reluctant engine and let the car idle for a minute to prepare it for another lunge into the world of real automobiles. "She told me that you wanted her to come."

Morris looked back at the little urchin. She smiled innocently.

"By the way," Heather said, "thanks for the mouse."

"Thank Fredo. He caught it."

"Why did he put it in a fish bowl?" asked Heather.

"I guess he wanted to teach it how to swim," Morris replied. Then, suddenly, he jumped up from his seat. "Wait a second, Heather," he shouted, "I forgot something!" And climbing over the passenger door, be bounded down onto the pavement.

"Moishe!" Heather shouted. "Where are you going?"

"I'll be right back!" he called out, dashing through the garden gate and hurrying up his stairs.

Inside the cottage he found a clean bowl and, rushing out again, he stopped at Arnold's garden where he pulled up a likely-looking plant, brushed off the roots and put it in the bowl. Then he went back to the waiting car.

"What's that, Moishe?" asked Rosa.

"Mary told me to bring a vegetable," he replied with a note of disgust.

Heather inspected it with a few sniffs and pokes. "It's rutabaga. I think it has to be cooked."

"No one's going to object as long as it's crunchy and grows in the ground," said Morris. "People nowadays would eat wrappings from the tomb of Tutankhamun if you could convince them it was organic."

Heather's car chugged down Army Street, that bleak, grey corridor which led to the freeway, letting off mechanical farts every thirty seconds or so. It was the way out of town. "To get to New York," Morris once told somebody heading for the Big Apple, "go down Army Street to the freeway. Keep eastbound over the bridge and stay on Highway 80 for three days."

The Farm, where they were headed, was adjacent to the freeway interchange. In the '60s it had been several acres of barren soil with a two-storey wooden-frame building. In the '70s it was taken over by some urban pioneers who used the smog-soaked land to grow their crops. The buildings became their community center. Morris saw it as a relic of the past; an anachronism in the atomized '80s. But it was surviving better than he was, so maybe he was wrong, he thought.

There was a cozy feeling inside when they arrived. He had pictured more gloom. Not out of sorrow, necessarily, but out of annoyance. Everyone had gone their own way. Morris felt that most of them didn't want to be reminded of the past. Or perhaps they didn't want to see their memories betrayed.

The warmth from the potbelly stove, stoked with sweetsmelling pine, took the chill out of the large, open room which, except for the colorful children's paintings on the wall, could easily have been mistaken for the dining-room of a Trappist monastery. The furniture was ascetic but functional — long wooden tables and long wooden benches. Morris rubbed his aching back and sighed.

Mary greeted them as they came in: "Hi, Heather, Morris — put your food on the table and join us. Hi, Rosa. Glad you came, too!"

Heather smiled. She liked Mary. Morris, on the other hand, wasn't sure he did. Mary was too officious for him. She was the type who blossomed when disaster struck. She needed something tragic to set her in motion. She wasn't a leader, she hadn't that sense of strategy. But she did know how to organize. Heather had always felt that Mary had been used. And perhaps that was true. But Morris thought it was just part of her character.

Rosa sidled up to Morris. "Are these your friends?" she asked in a whisper.

Morris felt a twinge. "Friends might be too strong a term," he said. He waved his hand toward the people around the potbellied stove. There were a few waves back.

Heather walked over to hug the congregation. Morris stayed by the table and opened a beer. He had hoped for something more alcoholic. Perhaps Roger had a flask, he thought. They had both liked alcohol better than dope.

As he considered the idea of approaching Roger, he felt a sharp nudge in his ribs. "Say, Moishe!" Rosa whispered emphaticially. "They just look like ordinary people!"

"What did you expect? A room full of Frankensteins?"

"No. Just not so ordinary, I guess."

"They look ordinary because they are ordinary, Rosa."

"Even then?"

"Well, no. They were a little nuttier then. You see that guy over there? The one that has a head like a punching bag?"

"You mean the balding guy with the round face?"

"Yeah. That's Irwin. He was beaten up more times than he can remember."

"How come?"

"He was organizing farm workers. That's why his nose is so flat. When I first knew him, he had a fine, aquiline schnoz."

"Who beat him up?"

"The grape farmers. They didn't like him going into their fields talking to their laborers."

"What does he do now?"

"I think he works with computers."

"How about that big guy over there?" Rosa pointed to a tall man with a trace of slouch who looked rather nervous. He kept shifting from one foot to another. Morris never knew whether it was his size or his frenetic movement which gave him such a strong presence. But once Roger came into the room, he was impossible not to notice.

"That's Roger," said Morris. "He was a pretty good speaker. He and I didn't agree all the time, but he was OK."

"Did he get beaten up a lot?"

"I don't think so. He was too smart for that."

"And what does he do now, Moishe?"

Morris realized he hadn't spoken with Roger for quite a while. "I don't know how he's earning a living, Rosa."

Rosa's big eyes surveyed the room, sucking everything in like a vacuum cleaner. "How about that lady talking with Heather? She looks pretty. Was she a commie, too, Moishe?"

He wondered whether she knew what that word meant. "Her name's Alice," Morris said. "She was a powerful speaker. She helped spark the anti-war movement."

"She looks like a dancer or an artist or something."

"She was — once upon a time. In fact, she was busted in an agitprop play."

"What for?"

"There was a law back then called 'Singing Obscenely in the Park'."

Rosa giggled. "Their singing sure must have been raunchy!"

"Yeah, they were accused of saying 'shit'."

Rosa caught her breath. "Really, Moishe? I say 'shit' all the time. I didn't know they could throw me in jail for saying it!"

"They just used it as an excuse, Rosa, because they didn't like what Alice was saying about the cops and the courts."

"Is she still acting?" Rosa looked up at him expectantly.

"I think she works for the telephone company now."

Rosa looked disappointed. "Oh."

Morris gave her a pat on the back. "Listen, Rosa, times are tough. So some of us drive taxis and some of us are clerks and some of us are telephone operators even though we wanted to be other things."

"Except for you, that is."

"Yeah, Rosa. Except for me. I'm just a bum."

She looked up at him apologetically. "Moishe, that's not what I meant."

Morris nodded. But he seemed almost grateful when Mary walked up to them and grabbed him by the hand. "Come on over, Morris. Don't be shy. We're having a reunion here. Did you and Heather have a spat or are you just waiting for a bus?"

She brought him over to where the others were standing. Rosa trailed along behind. Morris could hear Roger talking as they approached.

"I heard something interesting when I was down in Los Angeles last week."

"Something interesting in LA?" asked Bert with half a smile.

"A friend told me she went to the Vietnam symposium at UCLA and heard Rod Gipstein ranting about how the movement had actually prolonged the war by shouting too loudly."

"You mean God Ripstein is at it again?"

"Who's God Ripstein?" whispered Rosa to Morris.

"Rod Gipstein was one of the original founders of SDS," Morris whispered back in her ear.

"Remember when he flew this guy in from Germany to speak to us?" said Heather. "He tried to convince us that it was the duty of every red-blooded radical to join the Army, go to Vietnam, and instigate rebellion in the ranks."

"Yeah," said Mary. "I asked Rod when he was going to enlist and he showed me his deferment papers."

"He was always great at telling us where we went wrong," said Alice. "But I don't think I ever saw him on the picket line."

"Intellectuals don't walk picket lines. They've all got flat feet — just like cops," said Irwin.

Bert bit down on his pipe. "Not all intellectuals," he said. "Sartre sold *Le Cause de Peuple* on the streets of Paris at the age of sixty-five even though the paper was banned."

"What really gets my goat," said Heather, ignoring Bert's comment, "is that people like that are writing our history. They read the words of Lenin and thought they would play around with revolution just like kids nowadays play with computers. And when it didn't work, they blamed it on the movement."

"Morris wrote a book about 1968," said Irwin.

Morris cringed. Bert looked over at him. "Hey, Morris. I want to talk to you about that. You have some serious errors in there."

Morris nodded his head.

"Well, at least he wrote something," said Irwin. "All the other stuff about 1968 was written by people who went to fancy schools. Here we participated in the most important student strike in the country, and we're basically ignored because San Francisco State College trained teachers and accountants instead of nuclear physicists."

"Who cares?" said Alice. "We weren't doing it for the history books, Irwin. We were doing it to change things."

"In that respect we failed," said Bert, sucking on his pipe.

Alice looked at Bert in disbelief. "If Philip were here he would have taken that damn pipe of yours and stuck it in the potato salad!"

Suddenly the room fell quiet. It was the first time Philip's name had been mentioned and it seemed to throw them all off guard. It was as if Philip had actually entered the room, pushing his way into the conversation in that obnoxiously aggressive manner. Morris could almost hear him shout, "What about me? How come I wasn't invited to my own wake? What a bunch of crumbs! Here I am, the first one of us to die, and you don't even have the decency to let me in!"

But looking around the room, Morris could see that there was something else going on too. People's faces had changed. Their expressions had softened at the invocation of his name. Yet Philip was such a dislikable character it was hard to truly mourn his passing, and, of all the people, only Mary and Heather and Rosa (who hadn't even known Philip) showed the faintest sign of tears. Everyone else just looked slightly uncomfortable.

Still, Morris felt something was missing. There was a time when it was them against the world, when they all had to depend on one another. There was a time when they had their special handshakes and winks to help protect them from the daily barrage of media distortions and outright lies. But even then something was missing.

"They're trying to kill us off, you know," Morris heard himself say.

Suddenly he realized that all eyes were upon him.

"Who's trying to kill us off, Morris?" asked Irwin, looking at him suspiciously.

"I think he's speaking metaphorically," said Heather, throwing him a cautionary glance.

"I know what he means, though," said Alice. "It's the historical moment. But just think about the year before the strike. How many kids were with us? A handful! We were about as popular as the black plague. And then, one year later, we had them on our side, waiting to build the barricades."

"I'm not speaking metaphorically," said Morris. But he could have been talking to himself. No one seemed to hear him.

"It wasn't that we were such great organizers," said Bert. "We were catalysts, that's all."

"We were more than catalysts," said Heather. "We provided leadership."

"And where did we lead them?" asked Bert, in a challenging tone.

"To the administration building!" shouted Heather and Alice in unison. They looked at each other and laughed.

How often could they keep telling the same jokes and the same stories, Morris wondered? Probably till they were old and grey — if they lived that long, he thought. He knew now why he had been so reluctant to come. It was quite clear. They were still as cocksure and arrogant as ever. On the other hand, it was probably hard enough to survive without suffering his paranoia. And yet, what if he were right? What if they were being picked off, one by one? What could he tell them to do? Go to the police? Anyway, without any solid facts, they'd just think he was mad. Which brought up another point: perhaps he was.

"When was the last time you saw him?"

He looked up. It was Alice speaking and the question was directed to him. At least he thought it was since everyone else seemed to have drifted to other parts of the room.

"Seen who?" he replied.

"Philip. Isn't he the one we came here to remember?"

Morris shook his head. "I can't recall the last time I saw him. How about you?"

"Not for years."

"I wonder if any of us kept in touch with him . . . besides Mary, that is."

Alice popped open a beer and took a drink. "I think Roger saw him occasionally . . ."

He looked at her with surprise. "Really? Who told you that, Alice?"

She shrugged. "Maybe Roger told me himself."

Morris anxiously scanned the various clusters of people. "Do you see him anywhere?"

"You mean Roger?" asked Alice, looking at him curiously. "I think I saw him leave."

He was about to question Alice more closely when they were interrupted by Heather. She was accompanied by a slim, energetic man. It was Jeffery, his old nemesis.

Jeffery stuck out his hand. "Hey, Morris! Good to see you! I read your book. Can't say as I saw 1968 the same as you, but I enjoyed reading it. Listen, who was that guy with the red hair who liked to stuff his shirt down the toilet so the water would overflow? Was he one of us?"

Morris winced. "That's privileged information, Jeff. I can't divulge his name."

"Well, I remember the guy who bombed the telephone booth

98

outside the administration building," said Jeffery with a laugh. "That ain't a secret. But why did you write about such frivolous stuff?"

"Because, Jeff, it was the best of times, it was the worst of times; it was a serious struggle, it was a frivolous struggle."

"Do you want future generations to think about us like that, Morris? Is that what you really want?"

Morris looked at him. Jeffery was staring back into his eyes. Morris thought him as sanctimonious as a priest. "I don't know what I really want, Jeff. Do you?"

"Yes, I believe I do, Morris."

Heather lit up a joint. "Hey, come on you guys. Let's talk about something else." She handed the joint to Jeffery who took a toke and then passed it on to Morris.

"You don't smoke grass anymore?" asked Jeff with raised eyebrows.

"I've developed an allergy," said Morris handing it back to him. And then, as an aside to Heather, he muttered, "Did you see Roger leave?"

Heather shook her head before turning to join another little group.

"You got a cigarette?" asked Morris, looking back at Jeffery.

"I thought you gave it up," he said. "Didn't you say you were allergic?"

"To grass."

"Not tobacco?"

"Tobacco cured me of cancer, Jeffery. I was given two months to live. And then I started smoking again."

"I wouldn't be flippant about it, Morris. I've seen a lot of guys come in, young guys, just like you . . ."

"Into where?"

"The morgue," said Jeffery.

"The morgue?"

"Didn't you know? I went back to school. I'm a mortician now. Just finished my training. Next week I'm starting work in the Chicago mortuary," Jeffery said proudly. "I'm leaving day after tomorrow."

Morris stared at him. "That's disgusting, Jeffery. You should be ashamed of yourself!"

"What are you doing these days, Morris?" Jeffery said with a note of disdain.

"I lie in bed and smoke," said Morris.

"I wouldn't doubt it," said Jeffery. "While I'm helping to organize the morticians' union, you'll be polluting the air."

"That's better than necrophilia, Jeffery."

Jeffery checked to make sure that Heather wasn't within earshot. Then he winked. "You'd be amazed at some of the stiffs I've seen, Morris." And he made a curving motion with his hand, out from the top of his chest and then inward again.

"So why did you give up on San Francisco?" asked Morris. "I'm sure there's some great-looking corpses here."

"Too many drugs and too much kinky sex," said Jeffery. "This place is becoming another Sodom and Gomorrah."

Heather had returned with a roach in her hand. A seed was stuck in the end so it kept going out. She looked at Jeffery. "Can you light this?" she asked.

Morris took that as a cue and started to move toward the door. He had begun to feel as if he was suffocating inside this stuffy room. Outdoors it was cool. The fog was on its way, presaged by a drop in the temperature.

"It doesn't take long for that stove to heat the place up, does it?" A voice came from out of the night.

He looked around. Roger was sitting on a bench next to the shrubbery. He seemed to blend into the darkness. Morris walked over and sat down by his side.

"Haven't seen you around in a while," said Morris. "What have you been up to these days?"

Roger fingered his cigarette nervously. "I'm doing a little freelance writing. But it's just hand to mouth."

"Who are you writing for?"

"The *Nation*, the *Progressive*, *In These Times* — that's about it. And for what they pay, you might buy yourself a new typewriter ribbon."

"Alice said you saw Philip occasionally. That true?"

"I saw him now and then," said Roger, rubbing his hands together. His face looked strained.

"Got any ideas about the shooting?"

Roger shook his head. It was clear he wanted to change the subject. "How about yourself? How's your book doing?"

"Not so good," said Morris. "I'm expecting them to remainder it soon."

"Any chance of getting into paperback?"

There was a pained expression on Morris' face. "I don't think they've sold a thousand hardbacks yet."

"It's not a good time to be publishing our kind of stuff," said Roger. "Nobody buys books anymore."

"Some people must be buying books otherwise they wouldn't print them."

"Sure. Cookbooks, picture books, holiday guides. Let me ask you Morris, when was the last time you bought a new book?"

Morris shrugged. "I sold three to the Picaro last week — one by Agee, one by Deutscher, and one by Orwell."

"See what I mean? People like us write 'em and sell 'em. But who the hell buys 'em and reads 'em?"

"You got me. Maybe they trained a group of chimpanzees."

"Nowadays, if you want to write a book, you better aim it at the Quiche and Carriage trade," said Roger.

"Got a smoke?" asked Morris.

"Sure." Roger brought out a pack of Marlboros and flipped open the lid. Morris took one, lit up and then handed the cigarette back to Roger so he could light his own. "It used to be that you could write a book just for the libraries. Publishers figured they might break even on those sales alone."

"The libraries are closing," said Morris. The cigarette was returned to him and he took a long, luxuriant drag. "Haven't you heard? They're replacing them with Computer Link."

"That's another reason to stop writing books," Roger replied. "What people want now are short, snappy pieces — easy reading for commercial breaks; stuff that can be excerpted on the backs of cereal boxes. You know what I mean?"

Morris nodded. "There's always the exception. *Rameses' War Against the Hittites* seems to be doing well this year."

101

"You'd probably do better writing a book about the twelfth century BC than one about the '60s, Morris. But if you had to write it, you should have made it more academic."

"I don't think I could have done it," said Morris. "The '60s were too surreal."

"Not like the '30s, huh?"

"You carry a flask with you?" Morris asked. Roger shook his head. Morris sighed and continued on his train of thought. "The '30s and '40s were a straight road, right through World War II. The '50s were a climb through dark and spooky woods to the top of a haunted hill. And the '60s were a roller-coaster ride back down again. When I think of the '30s, I think of grim people who had a sense of destiny. When I think of the '60s, I think of Groucho Marx trying to organize a picket line. It wasn't very cerebral."

"You want a straight line?" asked Roger.

Morris rubbed his head. "No. I'm just tired of being depressed."

"I know what you mean," Roger said. "Times are tough."

"Hey, Moishe!" Heather called out. She was standing by the door. "I was wondering where you were." She came down to where the two men were sitting. "Jeff and I are going out for a drink. Can Rosa go home with you?"

"You mean you want her to sleep at my place?"

"Yeah, just for the night. Is that OK?"

"You want us to walk there?" His voice sounded resentful.

"You can have the car. Jeff has his own."

"Any gas in it? I don't have any money."

"I think there's enough, but here's a ten just in case." She reached into her purse and took out a bill. "Rosa's inside chatting with Mary. Thanks, Moishe. Hi, Roger. Bye, Roger."

Roger watched her in wonder as she rushed back inside. "Does she ever slow down? I mean she's been running since 1967."

"She's afraid to slow down. She thinks if she slows down she'll stop and then she won't be able to start up again. Like that damn car of hers!"

Roger got up and stretched his long arms. "I'm going back inside," he said. "Isn't this supposed to be a wake for Philip?"

Morris smiled. "Yeah. But people seem to have some trouble getting used to the idea that death is a fact of life."

"He's the first," Roger mused.

"There may be others," said Morris with an ominous note.

"Not too soon, I hope," said Roger, gazing down at his shoes. Then, looking back up at Morris, he said, "By the way, where's Fredo? I was hoping he'd come. He's doing pretty well for himself, I hear."

"He's got a couple of mysteries out," said Morris. "He's being read. Even making some dough. But it doesn't seem to have changed him much. He still lives in the same dump, still hangs out at the same places."

"Good for him!" said Roger.

Morris chuckled to himself. "Yeah, such a man of principle!"

"That's the name of the game," said Roger. "Try to get recognized and then use your leverage to get the good stuff published."

"Except by then you're too used to writing trash."

Roger laughed. "Do I detect a note of jealousy?"

"Maybe," said Morris. "But I've got something on the cooker that might really take off."

"What's it about?"

"I can't really talk about it now, Roger. It's still brewing."

"Yeah, I know what you mean," said Roger. "So where *is* Fredo? Why isn't he here?"

"He said he didn't feel like being a hypocrite. He didn't like Philip so he saw no reason to come to his wake."

"But they were comrades once," said Roger.

"Fredo doesn't buy that."

"He changed. Mellowed a bit."

"Who?"

"Philip. We were collaborating on an article, you know . . ."

There was a sudden zap of adrenalin that shot through his body. "No, I didn't. What was it about?"

"It was on the cooker."

"I see . . ." Morris felt Roger's anxiety begin to transfer itself to him. "Whose name were you writing under?" he asked.

Roger smiled meekly. "We wrote under the name of 'Mother Jones'. Hope you don't mind."

"You got another cigarette?" asked Morris.

"Take a couple," he said, holding out the box.

Morris took a few and put them in his shirt pocket. Lighting up, he said, "You remember a guy named Koba?"

There was a moment of silence. Then Roger said, "Why do you ask?"

"I got a call from him the other day," he said, studying Roger's reaction.

"That's very strange." Roger seemed to look past him into the darkness. "What did he say?"

"Nothing. He wanted to meet but he never showed up. Roger, I think something's up. We've got to talk."

Roger dropped his cigarette and ground it into the earth with the heel of his shoe. "Morris, I've got to go now," he said. "Can we meet tomorrow?"

"Where?"

"At the Café Commons on Mission and Precita. Can you make it around two?"

Morris nodded his head.

Chapter Eight

It was dark. His heart was beating fast. He could hear the sound — thump, thuda, thump, thuda, thump — deep within his chest. A sudden chill had come over him, as if someone had opened the door allowing the night air, the miasma, to seep in.

The sheets were wet. His body was soaking in cold sweat. He saw a shadow. It seemed to move toward him. Silently. His heart beat faster — thump, thump, thuda, thuda, thump. And then he realized the shadow had form, it had dimension. It was a man. A bony man. Dressed in a black coat and hat.

The figure came closer. He sensed that underneath the coat the body was gaunt and wasted, like the survivor of a concentration camp.

It came closer still. Now he could see the sallow skin and the darkness in the hollow eyes. And he recognized him. He knew who he was.

He whispered, "Why have you come?"

The figure said nothing. It stood there. Silently. And then it opened its cavernous mouth exposing a gaping black hole that stank of decay.

The voice was hoarse. The words came out slowly and painfully. "Can you see? I pulled them out. I pulled them out, one by one. Every tooth with metal. Every filling. So they couldn't broadcast anymore. But then one night they came again. They planted metal in my brain."

The figure bent its head and pointed to a bald spot where the skin was raw. It seemed like there were maggots in the flesh. "Look! They put it in while I was still asleep. I couldn't stop them." The voice became almost childlike now. It pleaded, "Can you help me, Morris? Can you help?"

He said, "Tell me what to do . . ."

105

The voice cried, "Take the metal out! Take it out before it's too late!"

"How can I do that?" he asked. "How can I take it out?"

He saw the thin lips smile. It was an evil smile. "You can take it out with this!"

And then he saw the bony hand that held the knife.

"No, Koba. I can't do that!"

The bony hand reached out. The knife blade flashed. The voice hissed: "Morris! You must die!"

He felt the knife blade in his heart. Thuda, thuda, thuda, thud. "That's it," he said. "I'm dead!"

She stuck her foot into his side again and twisted it so her toe worked through to his ribcage. "Come on, Moishe. It's after eleven already. Get up! I'm hungry!"

He opened his eyes and looked up at her. She had a determined look on her face. "And don't try to send me to school either! It's a holiday!"

"What are you doing here?" he moaned. And then he remembered. He buried his head in the pillow.

"Maybe we could go to the zoo," she said. "Or how about driving down to Santa Cruz? That might be fun!"

He let his head roll to the side. Two fingers opened his eyelids. "Hi down there!"

"Rosa," he said in a gravel-like voice, "there's a ten spot in my trousers. Run down to the Meat Market Café and get me a double espresso. OK?"

"Come on, Moishe. Just get out of bed. It's not hard. Then we can go to the Meat Market together."

"Rosa, I'm dying. Can't you see I'm dying?"

"If you don't get out of bed I'm going to tickle your feet!"

"Rosa, in some countries you can go to prison for torture."

She started tickling his feet. "Tickle, tickle, tickle . . ."

He lunged for her like a walrus going after a fish. She jumped backwards deftly. He landed in a heap on the floor.

"Now that you're up, you want me to get you your pants?"

Coffee helped; it usually did.

"So you'll let me spend the day with you?" she asked hopefully.

"Maybe part of the day," he replied. If caught while the caffeine was still coursing through his veins, he was a sucker for anything. "I need to see someone."

"You got a hot lead, Moishe?"

"Hot lead? I don't even have a cold hint, Rosa. Did you bring your swimming suit with you?"

"Swimming suit? The someone that you got to see — he ain't a fish, is he?"

"Well, you know what they say. If you're looking for a fish, try asking a fisherman."

"Who says that, Moishe?"

He gave her a look. "Grab your hat," he said. "Let's go!"

The sun was out, drying the dampness of the morning's fog. They drove down Dolores Street to Market where they veered right. The great stone edifice of the San Francisco Mint dominated the corner. Morris had always wondered whether there could possibly be a moat surrounding it. One could only see the sheer cliff and the barbed-wire fence from this perspective. The walkway to the entrance of the Mint was obscured from view. He supposed there could have been a moat. And even a dragon. The government, he felt, would go to any length to protect its money.

They went down Market only a short way before turning left up Franklin Street. As they approached Civic Center, they passed the new symphony hall (a glass mausoleum to the barons of culture, Morris called it) and the Opera House where the elite met the sweet, and bored-to-hell old men slept in fancy clothes. On the other side of Franklin Street the Western Addition was being torn down. Morris ruminated. "Gentrification" they called it. The Blacks were being shifted further south. Maybe all the way to Alabama, for all he knew. Morris always wondered where the poor went after they were dispossessed. It wasn't as if they were building any apartments to house them. Maybe they just dug another hole with the same bulldozers that tore down their homes and pushed them in. That wouldn't have surprised him. He thought of reading the headlines in the *San Francisco Chronicle* one day: "Hundreds of bodies found in excavation site! Authorities at loss to explain!"

They continued up Franklin Street and then down the other side. At the bottom of the hill was the Marina. On a clear day like this, with just a trace of mist rising from the Bay, it was like a Mediterranean fantasy. From here you could almost taste the azure blue of the water. The effect was like a powerful drug on his worn psyche.

At Bay Street they turned left again, skirting the grounds of Fort Mason, and then onto the majestic highway that led toward the Golden Gate Bridge. Marina Boulevard ran like a ribbon between the small-craft harbor and the row of million-dollar showplaces that lined the road on the other side.

Rosa was hanging out the side of the car, long hair flying like the tail of a kite. Tears rolled down her cheeks from the force of the wind. Her face was glowing.

Morris wondered at how easily she cried. It wasn't that he minded; in fact, he quite envied her. There was a time that he, himself, could cry. Nowadays he couldn't even get tears from peeling onions.

They parked the English Ford by the Yacht Club and then strolled along the path that once had been the finest walk in town before the joggers had discovered it was runable.

The tide was out which meant the expanse of sandy beach was wide enough to avoid those that Morris referred to as "The Giraffes".

"Why do you call them giraffes?" asked Rosa.

"Because their necks grow longer each time they run. Watch them yourself. They look like panicked animals hoofing through the forest. They stretch their necks in fear because someone told them if they ever stop running, they'll die. Now they run together in packs. It's the herding instinct. Fortunately there isn't a cliff out there because they'd keep running until they fell into the sea. This way they just run till they hit a wall or something."

The small boats were out in the bay, playing with the currents. The multicoloured sails painted the ocean with their hues. Across the water, the wheat-colored hills of Marin slumbered quietly in the sun.

"Moishe!" exclaimed Rosa. "You're smiling!"

He looked at her with amusement. "You've never seen me smile before?"

"Not lately," she said. She grinned back at him and began skipping down the beach.

He remembered walking here years ago with Heather. It was right after the promenade had been constructed. Before then it had been part of the Presidio and was reserved for the Army. Few people knew about the place when it was first liberated. In those days it was quiet. He and Heather could walk undisturbed from the Yacht Harbor to Fort Point which sat below the Golden Gate Bridge on the other end. And they marveled at the grandeur that had been hidden from them all those years.

"Where's the fish?" she asked, skipping back to him.

"What fish?"

"The fish you needed to meet."

"He's over there." Morris pointed in the direction of an old fisherman dressed in a bright yellow slicker and matching boots. The top of his head was hidden under a blue seaman's cap. He was smoking a pipe.

The fisherman squinted his eyes as Morris waved.

"You mean in that guy's net?" she asked.

"Could be."

They walked over to where the fisherman was standing. As they came near, the old guy pointed out toward a ship sailing in under the gate. "Look at that!" he said, a sour expression on his face. "Another blasted container ship! That's the third one I've seen today!"

"Hey, Curly," Morris called out. "I knew I'd find you here!" He grabbed Curly's extended hand and gave it a shake. Turning to Rosa, he said, "Curly was my partner back in the days when I used to work the docks."

"Nice lookin' girl," he said, winking at the child. "'Course I'd be here, Kaplan! Where the hell else would I be?"

"I don't know, Curly. I thought maybe you decided to come out of retirement and start working the docks again."

"No. You got it all wrong." Curly shook his head. "See, they retired me. They retired half the guys. You know that, Morris.

There ain't no work out there." He pointed to the container ship. Morris nodded.

Rosa was fingering the long pole stuck in the ground. "You catch any fish?" she asked him.

Curly turned to look at her. "Naw, honey. I never catch any fish. It just gives me an excuse to sit here. I hate to do nothing."

"Nothing?" Morris clucked his tongue. "Say, I thought you were going to open a restaurant!"

"Me?" Curly laughed. "You must be thinkin' of Maxie. Maxie opened a bar out on 3rd Street. Down by China Basin. Doin' pretty well till they raised the rent and kicked him out. Now he's a rummy like the rest of us."

"Come on, Curly. I remember the chiappino you used to make." He looked at Rosa. "This guy made the best crab stew in the world! Be nice to him and maybe he'll invite you over for dinner."

Curly looked confused. "Sure, I'll invite you over. Ain't got much though. Crab's too expensive these days. Last time I looked it was three-fifty a pound. Imagine that! Three-fifty a pound! Christ, we used to pick 'em up for fifty cents!"

"I'm just joking, Curly. I wouldn't impose on you."

"No. I like company. I don't get much company any more. Sometimes I even go over to that old folks' place in the Maritime Museum just so's I can find someone to play cards with."

Morris stared at the man who had taught him to unload ships. He had aged in the last ten years. Now he seemed old. His eyes were baggy and his cheeks were sallow. Morris wondered how he looked to Curly.

It was in 1969 that he and Curly had met. The word had gone out that the ILWU, the dockers' union, would take on some of the striking professors as casual workers. Some of the graduate students would get "B" cards, too. In fact, half the guys from SDS ended up down on the docks, working with the very people they someday hoped to organize.

Morris felt young and strong back then. On his first day, he unloaded sacks of cocoa beans from the *Paloma Queen* out of Brazil. The gunnysacks weighed in at close to 100 pounds each. Morris had tried to lift one and had collapsed to his knees.

A bald man with thick grey eyebrows shook his head and chuckled. "They didn't teach you that in philosophy class, did they, son?"

Morris had looked at him helplessly.

Curly had leaned down and whispered, "It's all in knowing how to lift, kid. You're strong enough. You must have seen pictures of them Vietnamese women. They carry two of these sacks at a time."

He gave Morris his extra hook. "I always carry two. Just for kids like you. It's leverage that you need, son. Those sacks are too ungainly to lift over your shoulder like that. The weight shifts and you lose your balance. Use your hook. That way you have something solid to hang on to."

Morris had lunch with him that first day. Curly took him to the Eagle Café, an old ramshackle place located on the Embarcadero that shook its weather-worn timbers every time the old Belt Line railroad lumbered into service.

They drank Millers and had a couple of ham and cheeses on sourdough French rolls. It was Curly's eyes that had fascinated him. His face may have been wrinkled, but the eyes were young. They twinkled when he spoke.

He found himself on Curly's crew a good number of times as the months went by. Maybe Curly had an in with the dispatcher. Morris never knew. They never spoke about it. But they became friends. Sometimes they would just hang out on the docks, talking about the "old days".

Curly had been a dock worker since the beginning of time. He was one of the originals. He had probably been there when the first clipper ships had rounded Cape Horn on their perilous passage to the gold country.

He took Morris to the shrine of the dock workers, the place that used to be Rincon Hill and now was the city's main post office. It was here, Curly said, that the cops fired the shots that set San Francisco aflame. It was during the height of the Great Strike of 1934. The men were walking the picket line along with the women of the workers' auxiliary. By midday two men lay dead on the ground. They died, Curly said, because they had the dignity to stand fast. The cops had killed them but their blood ran

111

through the city's streets, seeping under the doors of the bakeries, the butcher shops and the finest hotels. Within the week, the city had been shut down. And the greatest general strike that America had known was suddenly capturing headlines throughout the world. The workers were waving the red flag, said Curly, and the cops had shouldered their billy clubs. So what if it only lasted a few days? It was a moment in history to be savored. And Curly licked his lips.

Morris had invited him to some SDS meetings. Curly had laughed. "I don't understand you kids," he said. "I don't know why you let you hair grow long or why you smoke pot. In fact, I think most of you are lazy bums who dream the world owes you a living."

"Some of us want to change the world so it does owe us a living instead of us owing Matson Shipping Lines a living."

"Well, you ain't gonna get that by busting things up. You got to have a plan. You got to have the workers behind you. Why the hell don't you cut your hair?"

"What difference does it make how long my hair is?"

"Because the workers won't listen to a punk kid with long hair, that's why."

"Curly, you're just jealous," he said, patting the old man's bald top.

That was fourteen years ago. Morris had stayed on the docks four more years, till the US had finally decreed that no more armaments were to go to Vietnam. Then the docks shut down once again. Not from workers' action, but from lack of trade.

"Curly and I fought the war together," Morris told Rosa.

"Were you in the war? What war was that?" Rosa looked confused.

"The war to end all wars, kid," Curly chuckled.

"We fought the war of the docks, honey. We declared that no piece of machinery would be shipped to Vietnam from a San Francisco port unscathed. Any vehicle bound there got a dose of sugar in the gas tank. All carburetors got a squirt of epoxy. Tires got the hook. We wrote slogans on every carton and stuffed in letters for the GIs telling them of the war resistance back home."

112

"That's one of the reasons the war ended, kid. It was the quiet stuff that took place. The stuff that no one ever talked about. Not those dumb marches that real workers never took part in."

"The marches helped, too," said Morris. "They helped mobilize people and build resistance."

"You build resistance by getting workers at the point of production," Curly shot back. "When the workers are ready to march, they'll march. That's when a march means something. When everything stops. A bunch of kids and old ladies marching means nothing at all."

"Well, you better not tell Heather that," said Rosa. For the first time that day she felt offended.

"Pardon an old man, kid." Curly smiled. "I don't know what the hell I'm saying anymore. You listen to your dad here. He's a smart man. He's been to college . . ."

Morris blushed.

Curly stuck out a calloused hand. "Wanna shake? No offense?"

Rosa took his finger and shook it firmly.

"That's the ticket, kid! Keep a stiff upper lip! Don't let old codgers like me turn you around."

"You're not an old codger," she said. "I like you. I just don't think you should be down on children and old women."

Curly laughed and slapped Morris on the back. "Quite a kid you got there. I bet she don't let you get away with much yourself!"

"Not much," Morris agreed. And then, looking into Curly's eyes, he said, "Did you ever run into a guy named Koba? He worked down at the docks for a while."

The old man rubbed his chin. "Strange name. It sounds familiar, but my memory's none too good nowadays. Who is he?"

"Someone I once knew," said Morris.

"You in trouble, son?" asked Curly.

Morris shrugged. "Strange things have been happening lately."

"I know what you mean," said Curly. "It just ain't the same no more, is it?"

"A friend of mine was bumped off the other day," said Morris, making a pattern in the sand with the toe of his shoe.

"Probably drugs," said Curly. "Everyone's being stiffed because of drugs these days."

Morris chuckled. "Not everyone, Curly."

"In my day it was booze," said Curly, ignoring his reply. "Now no one smuggles booze — it's drugs. There's so much coming in these days they could probably open up the docks again and hire half the city if it weren't for the fact they have to keep it down."

"How does the stuff come in?" asked Morris.

"Every way you can think of," said Curly. "In China dolls and sacks of flour. But the important stuff that gets in could probably be packed in plastic bags."

"What do you mean?" asked Morris.

"It's all a fix," said Curly. "It's the drugs that ain't going through the proper channels that gets nixed."

"You know anyone I could talk to inside the drug trade?"

"Me?" Curly shook his head. "Nah. I stay away from that stuff and if you had any sense you would too. It's bad trouble, Kaplan. Too much money changes hands. Even decent sorts of people begin losin' their perspective when so much dough like that starts flyin' around." Then he hesitated for a minute and looked out to sea. "Funny you should ask, though . . ."

"Why's that, Curly?"

"It's maybe nothin', but, you know, sometimes you pick up things without meanin' to."

"Yeah, I know. What kind of things are you picking up, Curly?"

"Just seems like there's a lot of edginess around the docks these days. Reminds me of the prohibition years, right before a mob war."

"What do you mean?"

"It was a mood more than anything else. One day you'd get this feeling, then the next day you read in the press that three or four bodies were found floating in the deep. Then it was over and everything went on just the way it went before."

"What happened, do you think?"

114

"Maybe a change of alliances. Maybe a few people weeded out. Who knows? Same thing happens in all business, I guess, only in the straight world they don't always use guns."

Suddenly Curly's fishing line started to tug. Rosa was the first to notice. Her face lit up and she grabbed Curly by the sleeve. "Hey! You got a fish, Curly! Quick, pull it in before it gets away!"

"It's nothing, kid. Maybe it's a piece of driftwood or an old shoe. Nobody ever catches anything here. That's why it's so relaxing."

"Aren't you even going to pull it in?" she asked with a note of amazement.

"Naw. What's the use?"

"Come on, Curly! I want to see! Even if it is an old shoe. I still want to see! Please?"

Curly shrugged his shoulders and pulled in the line. It was a lump of green seaweed on the other end. Curly cursed under his breath. "See, kid, you should never had made me pull it in. That way neither of us would have been disappointed." He turned to Morris. "Damn kids nowadays have no respect. No respect at all!" He sat down in the sand and stared out into the bay.

Rosa gave Morris a troubled look. He winked back at her, leaned down next to Curly and put an arm around his shoulder. "Nice running into you, Curly. Let's keep in touch, OK?"

Curly looked up. It was as if he just recognized him. "Oh, sure. I'll see you soon. Give me a call, huh? Maybe we'll have a beer at the Eagle."

"That would be great! I'll look forward to it. See you soon, Curly." Morris gave him a pat on the back. Then he took Rosa's hand and started to walk back down the beach. But Rosa pulled away. She went over to the old man and knelt beside him.

"Goodbye, Curly," she said. "Sorry things are a little rough." She smiled and gave him a kiss on his cheek. Curly looked up at her pretty face. And Morris thought he saw those old hollow eyes glisten again.

Chapter Nine

Morris arrived at the Café Commons precisely at two. The place was already packed. He didn't like meeting people here. It was too crowded; you never knew when a stranger would decide to sit at your table and eavesdrop. Not that they did it on purpose, of course — there was just nowhere else to sit. And once they sat down, they weren't going to put on earmuffs.

It was two-thirty when Roger finally showed. He doffed his hat and, looking at Morris apologetically, said, "I'm sorry. I got hung up." And then he added, "It was business," as if that were more of an excuse.

"Not to worry," said Morris. "I was reading *In These Times*. They keep it here, stapled to a rack and hung up on the wall."

"I can't stay too long," said Roger. "You want something to drink?" He appeared even more haggard than usual this afternoon. His large frame seemed to bend in the middle, like a weighty tree after a wind storm.

"A coffee," said Morris. "Make it a double espresso."

Roger came back in a few minutes with two steaming brews. "I can't drink much espresso anymore. It gives me the shakes," he said.

"It gives me the shakes if I don't," said Morris, taking a sip.

Roger had the appearance of a man standing on the bow of a sinking ship. Perhaps the half-tragic air that Morris had sometimes noticed was a function of size — being trapped within a powerful frame without having the coordination that usually came with it.

"I'm sorry I had to run off last night," he said, smiling nervously. He looked across at Morris without actually meeting his eyes. "When did you hear from him?"

"Koba?"

116

He nodded his head.

"Just a few days ago. He didn't say anything except that he wanted to meet me. He said he'd come to La Bohème that afternoon. He didn't keep the appointment, but . . ." Morris hesitated before going on.

Roger fingered his cup. His eyes darted around the room. "But what?"

"Something happened outside La Bohème. An old woman standing next to me was shot."

"And you think Koba . . ." Roger's voice trailed off. He began nervously biting his lip.

"Who else? Roger, what kind of article were you and Philip collaborating on? Did it have anything to do with Koba?"

"In a way . . ."

Morris sighed. "Was it about drugs?"

"More than that . . ." Roger glanced around the room again and then lowered his voice. "It had to do with something big, Morris. Something really big!"

Morris sensed a gleam in Roger's eye. "Big enough to get Philip shot?"

Roger put his hand over his face and slowly shook his head. "Jesus, I don't know."

"Come on, Roger!" Morris whispered emphatically. "I think Koba's out to get us, damn it! You have to tell me whatever you know!"

"But Morris, that's just it!" said Roger, giving him a startled look. "Koba's dead!"

"That's what Rocky said . . ."

Roger showed his surprise by raising an eyebrow. "You spoke to Rocky Calhoon?"

"Yeah. He told me Koba had been killed in Bolivia. Is Rocky in on this too?"

"We were using him for legal advice," he admitted.

"So what's it about, Roger? Are you going to trust me or not?"

"It doesn't have anything to do with trust," said Roger. "It's just that I'm in pretty deep and I don't want to get you involved."

He felt like shaking him. "Are you kidding? Getting shot at isn't involved enough for you?"

117

Roger began drumming his fingers on the table. "I don't understand that at all."

"So why don't you let me know what's going on," said Morris with exasperation. "Maybe I can help."

"It's too dangerous," said Roger, shaking his head once more. "It's got to do with the CIA, the Mafia, everything . . ."

Watching Roger's nervous ways, Morris was getting jittery himself. It was that uncomfortable, clammy feeling again, like the symptoms of an unpleasant disease. If this were years ago, he could have shrugged it off. Danger was all around then. But now these feelings seemed to be out of sync with the times.

Morris recalled the old Roger — quick, nervous, always on the go. But then it was combined with an inexhaustible energy and a self-assured air. Now he looked more like a man about to fit his neck into a hangman's noose. And there were so few things left to die for.

"You really think Koba's alive?" Roger asked, almost hopefully.

"I know he's alive," Morris responded.

"If Koba were alive it would change everything," said Roger.

"Listen to me, Roger," Morris said, trying to meet his eye. "I know someone who might be able to help us out."

"Who?"

"Someone who can find out about Koba for us."

All at once Roger seemed to come to life again. "OK, find out anything you can!" he said, getting up from his chair. "It doesn't matter how trivial it seems — anything might be important now!" He tore a slip of paper from his notebook and handed it to Morris. "Here's my number. Call me after you speak to your friend!"

Morris stared up at him. "Where are you running off to, Roger? Aren't you going to tell me what it's all about?"

"Soon," said Roger. And, as an afterthought, he said, "Listen, if anything happens to me, get ahold of Rocky."

"Does he have a copy of the article?" asked Morris.

Roger nodded his head. Suddenly he smiled. "Almost like old times again, isn't it?" And then he turned and hurried away.

*

The notion of having dinner with Heather and Jeffery didn't send him into a state of wild ecstasy. But hunger, and the thought of eating at his favorite restaurant again, compliments of a mortician-to-be, won out.

"Jeff insists," Heather had said when he talked to her on the phone. "He says he can afford it now. Besides, he wants to talk to you about something."

He met them at US Restaurant on Columbus and Stockton in the heart of North Beach. Morris and Heather had gone there for years, whenever either of them had an extra buck. But it had been many months since he had satisfied his appetite for a good home-cooked Italian meal, partly because of his self-imposed diet but mainly due to a lack of funds.

"Is this place so great that we have to stand in line?" Jeffery asked. He was anxious to sit down.

"Yeah," said Heather, "it is."

"We can share a table," Morris suggested.

"Let's see if something comes up in the back room," Heather said. "It's quieter."

The building was what would have been called "flatiron" in New York City. It was a triangular structure built into the merging of Columbus and Stockton Streets. The back room of the restaurant fit snugly into the apex of the angle. One table was squeezed neatly into the nook before the building disappeared.

Morris remembered when the back room had been an Italian travel office. He would pass the place with a wistful glance at the ancient steamships on the posters. It seemed they were all heading to Italy — Genoa, Naples, Brindisi. Magical names to think about while eating pasta and fazool.

A table finally opened up. Morris ordered his favorite meal — a bowl of clam chowder followed by halibut with tomato sauce, polenta, and a glass of chianti. Heather opted for an order of calamari and pasta al pesto. Jeffery ordered pot roast.

"You should have some of this, Jeff," Morris said while slurping his chowder. "It's only fifty cents more."

Jeffery smiled benevolently. "It's not the money, Morris. I just don't like fishy stuff."

Muttering something under his breath, Morris continued spooning his soup.

Heather took a drink of wine and looked at Morris. "Jeff offered me a job in Chicago," she said.

Morris responded by gagging on a piece of bread.

Heather patted him on the back. "Are you all right?" she asked.

He stared at her incredulously. "You want to work in a mortuary?"

"The union is hiring an organizer, Morris. I thought Heather would be perfect for the job. She's dying on the vine here. She needs something challenging in her life." Jeffery ended his sentence with a patronizing smile.

Morris glared at him. "What makes you think Chicago would be better for her than San Francisco?" Turning to Heather, he asked, "Have you talked to Rosa about this?"

Heather shook her head. "I mentioned the idea to her this evening. But it's silly for me to talk too much about it with her before I've thought it out myself."

"Why?" asked Morris. "She might have some ideas on the subject."

"She's a child," Jeffery scolded. "That's one of the problems. She hasn't been made to understand that."

Morris ignored him. He kept looking at Heather. "Why didn't you speak to me about this before?"

"I just brought up the idea yesterday," said Jeffery.

Heather shrugged and started to eat her meal again. Morris looked back at Jeffery. That stupid smile seemed to be painted on his lips. And then, like a Cheshire cat, his face began to blur and fade from sight till all that was left was the ridiculous grin.

They finished their dinner without many more words being spoken. Morris felt a stomachache brewing. He wasn't sure whether it was the rich food or Jeffery's company that did it to him.

Heather offered to drive him back to his cottage but Morris told her he had business in North Beach that night. In fact, he just wanted to be left alone. He started walking down Columbus Avenue but when he reached the corner of Broadway, the overwhelming feeling of nausea suddenly erupted. And he threw up, there and then, all over the streets of his spiritual home. What annoyed him most was the waste of a good meal.

It was well past midnight when Morris heard the knock at his door. He got up from his desk, pushing his papers to one side, and answered it. Jack seemed to hover in the doorway for a moment before coming in, as if he found it difficult to go from darkness into light.

He was carrying a shopping bag that he put atop the table. "You like Chinese food?" he asked, taking out an assortment of wax-coated cardboard containers.

Morris averted his eyes as Jack opened a carton of won ton soup and began to fish for the meat filled doughy things with his chopsticks. Somehow it reminded Morris of a cop dredging for a corpse in a polluted pond.

"Dig in!" said Jack. "I brought enough for an army!"

"I ate," said Morris. "You bring any smokes?"

Jack pointed to the bag. "There's a bottle inside too. I noticed we finished yours the other night."

Morris took out the pack of Chesterfields and the bottle of whisky. He lit up a smoke and poured out two glasses, passing one to Jack, who, by now, had finished the soup and was starting on his chicken chow mein.

"I found out something about Koba for you," said Jack.

Morris took a drink of whisky. "Was he one of yours?"

Jack looked up from his food. "He was — once. It seems we had him positioned in a drug network, but somehow he was fingered. So we let the word go out that he was dead. Then something happened. We lost track of him."

"And now he turns up here. What does he want from us, Jack? We haven't seen him for years!"

"I don't know, Morris." Jack wiped his mouth with a paper napkin and then looked Morris in the eye. "Unless it has something to do with an article some friends of yours were writing."

"You know about the article?" Morris said with some surprise.

"Nothing except what I picked up from my sources. What do you know about it?"

"Not much except that it links Koba and drug smuggling."

"Maybe Koba found out . . ."

Morris rubbed the side of his face and thought a minute. "Do you think we're in danger, Jack?"

"You very well could be. If it has something to do with the article, that is . . ."

He hesitated before he said it. "Do you think we should go to the cops?"

"That wouldn't do any good," said Jack. "They wouldn't believe you."

"But they'd believe you," said Morris.

Jack smiled. "You don't know the Company like I do, Morris. I'd disappear a minute after I went there."

"Disappear?"

"Without a trace."

Morris shook his head. "So what do we do, Jack? We can't just sit here and let Koba bump us off — one by one."

"Why don't you let me handle it," said Jack. "I think I know what to do. Who was the other 'Mother Jones'?"

Morris hesitated.

"Let me have his name and address," said Jack.

He felt a lump in his throat.

"Every second counts. Koba struck once. He'll strike again."

He tried to speak but nothing came out of his mouth.

"What's wrong?" asked Jack, looking at him intently.

Morris stared back. "How come you left the CIA? You never did tell me . . ."

Jack stroked the bristles of his cheek and looked down. "Did you ever hear of the death squads, Morris?"

"You mean the right-wing groups in Latin America who make people disappear? What about them?"

"They're very evil people who operate with impunity, Morris. They're quite skilled at crushing revolutionary ideals. Do you know the sort of things they do?"

"I can imagine."

"No. You can't imagine, Morris. Your imagination is far too

limited. But I'll give you an example of their technique. There was once an active revolutionary — his name is unimportant, let's call him José Y. One day he was kidnapped by the death squad and taken to a deserted house. There he was kept in a room where he was tied to a chair and questioned about his contacts. He was tortured, but he didn't speak . . ."

"Good for him," said Morris.

"Anybody can be made to speak," said Jack. "Anybody."

"Yes, I suppose they can."

"To make someone speak isn't difficult. What takes a little more imagination is how totally to crush someone's faith. The death squads are quite proficient at this, however. Like in the case of José Y. He didn't speak, you see. So one day they brought his daughter — a lovely girl of some twelve or thirteen years. She was the apple of his eye . . ."

"I don't think I want to hear any more," said Morris.

"You have to hear this," said Jack. "I want you to understand how far they can go."

"I can guess."

"No. You have no idea, Morris. The girl was raped right in front of him. And, of course, he told them everything. He told them everything there was to say. But that wasn't all . . ."

"What else did they want?"

"They wanted to crush him, Morris. They wanted to crush all hope."

"So they killed him. Is that what you're getting at?"

"No," said Jack. "You don't understand at all. They killed her. They slit her open with a knife. They butchered her just like a little lamb. And they forced him to watch."

Morris felt the taste of bile in his mouth. The words jammed up in his throat. "Why are you telling me this, Jack?" he managed to say.

"After they were finished, they gave him a gun with one bullet in the chamber . . ." Jack hesitated for a moment. "What would you have done, Morris, if someone raped and butchered your daughter right in front of you? What would you have done with that gun? Would you have stuck it in your mouth and killed yourself? Or would you have shot one of them?"

Morris let out a sigh of disgust. "I don't know, Jack. I don't know what I'd do if they cut off my arms and legs and threw me in the ocean or hacked up Heather or ground Rosa into sausage meat. You can't prepare for things like that in life." He looked back into Jack's eyes. "What did he do?"

"I don't know, Morris. But what I do know is that the gun they gave him had only one bullet — and that bullet was a blank."

"A blank?"

"A fiendish stroke of brilliance, wouldn't you say? They forced him to live, Morris. They wanted his life as a testament to their power. They wanted hope to be forever crushed."

For a moment the room was silent. Then Jack said, "Give me his name, Morris. These people are ruthless. Give me his name before it's too late."

Morris reached inside his pocket and took out the slip of paper Roger had given him. It was wet from the sweat of his fingers. "His name is Roger Billings. Here's his phone number and address. I'm worried about him, Jack."

"What did he tell you about his research?" asked Jack.

"Not much."

Jack got up from his chair and started putting all the empty containers into his shopping bag. Then he wiped the table clean. "I'll contact you tomorrow," he said, taking the bag and walking to the door.

"Can't I contact you?" asked Morris.

"It's better if I contact you," said Jack. "And remember, it's important that my visits remain unnoticed." He opened the door. Standing in the doorway, half in darkness, half in light, he said, "And, Morris, one thing more — be sure to lock up well tonight."

Chapter Ten

Morris tried Roger's number again. Getting no response, he left the receiver off the hook, allowing it to ring while he searched the cupboard for something to eat. He knew he wouldn't find anything, but he checked again just to make certain. Perhaps, he thought, Rosa had hidden a jar of peanut butter, like a squirrel hides its acorns for the winter.

The meal last night had whetted his appetite even though he couldn't keep it down. And now he was starting to have food fantasies again. He dreamed of steak smothered in mushrooms, a side-order of mashed potatoes swimming in gooey butter, a glass of beer and a good cigar.

He checked the telephone once more to see if Roger had picked up his end and then, still hearing the ring, walked outside onto the porch. It was nearly eleven o'clock. The sun was bright. Arnold's garden, basking in the warming rays, was as neat and trim as a well-kept table. And it seemed to be beckoning like a snake in the Garden of Eden.

Gazing down at the vegetable patch, he felt his stomach start to rumble. He despised vegetables. But hunger won out. And his feet, acting on their own, carried him down to the rows of tilled earth penetrated by tender shoots of sweet-smelling food. So what if Arnold would have killed to protect his organic children? He reached down and pulled out bunches of carrots, and radishes. He picked a handful of tomatoes and cucumbers from their vines. He tried to cover his tracks by smoothing the soil, but he was too hungry to be really careful.

He ran back up to his cottage with the agility of a teenager in heat. He kicked the door shut behind him, scurried across the room and threw the vegetables into an empty bowl. He didn't even bother to wash them. After all, Arnold was an organic farmer. And even though the garden had been smothered in manure, at least it was natural. It didn't make any difference anyway. By now Morris wouldn't have cared if he had found them in a sewer.

It was an orgy. He stuffed his mouth full of radishes and washed them down with cucumber and tomato. He chewed a carrot for dessert. It was fantastic! And it filled his mind with strange new visions of orange-robed women with daisies in their hair dancing through wheat fields in the spring.

Then he thought of Jeffery.

He barely made it to the toilet in time. And, afterward, he sat there on the enamel throne, regretting his rash behavior. It was like expiating his sins. He kept repeating, "I swear to God, I promise never to eat another vegetable again. Just let me live!" His pleas were answered. But by then he had already reverted to his agnostic sensibilities.

When he stumbled back toward his bed, he noticed that the receiver was off the hook. He picked it up. It was still ringing. "Damn!" he thought. He had been trying to call Roger since early that morning. Well, early to him anyway. He had started at ten, thinking that Roger, being a writer, would have stayed in bed until at least that hour.

Then he thought that perhaps he had written down the number incorrectly when he copied it from the slip Roger had handed him. And since he had given the original to Jack last night, he had no way to check it out. So he decided to phone Mary; she had everyone's current address and telephone number neatly filed on Rollidex cards. She would know.

Mary's voice sounded strange when she answered the phone. He didn't recognize it at first.

"Mary, is that you?"

"Oh, Morris! You've heard! Isn't it terrible? First Philip, now Roger . . ."

Morris felt a pain in his chest. "Mary, don't joke with me."

"How could you accuse me of joking about something like that, Morris? Roger's dead!"

"Mary . . ." His voice was shaking. "Don't go away! I'll be right there!"

She shouted, "Morris! Wait!"

He hung up the phone and ran out the door.

He kept telling himself to calm down. It was well enough to say, but how do you tell a chemical anything? Something had been released in his bloodstream and it was making his heart pound like a racehorse pumped up with steroids.

He was running fast, but his feet were numb. His ears had blocked out the screeching of horns as he raced across the streets. He couldn't even hear the squeal of brakes or see the angry drivers shake their fists through open windows. But they were in a separate world. He was running for his life. They were in their shells and had no idea of the terror that was driving him. So they shouted out of anger, because they couldn't understand. They thought he was a malcontent defying the rules of traffic. How could they have known that he felt he had just moments left to live?

Mary was waiting at her door. She lived on Elizabeth Street between Castro and Noe. It was only a ten-minute walk from Morris' place. Today he had run it in five.

"I was about to leave," she said. "What's gotten into you?"

"What's gotten into me?" he shouted. "You tell me that Roger's dead and now you ask what's gotten into me?" He glared at her with wild eyes.

"Calm down, Morris. I know it's terrible. But you're not going to help anyone by flying off the handle. Come on inside. I'll open a beer."

Morris was beginning to feel light-headed. He barely was able to climb the stairs, his feet were so wobbly. "Could you fix me a sandwich, too?" He could hardly recognize his own voice.

"Sure, Morris. What do you want? Is cheese all right?"

"Anything — as long as it's not vegetables."

"What?" She was already in the kitchen, slicing up the ingredients. "You want lettuce?"

"No!"

"Mayo? Mustard? Chives?"

Who was she, he wondered? Julia Child? "Just cheese between two slices of bread will be fine."

She brought it out on a plate, complete with napkin, fork, and toothpick. The toothpick was stuck into the sandwich, supposedly to hold the two slices of bread together. He didn't know what the fork was used for.

She opened a beer and poured it into two glasses. She handed one to him.

"Great cheese," he said, stuffing his mouth full. "Where'd you get it?"

"At the grocer's."

She sat down and watched him devour the food.

The meal seemed to revive him. The panic had subsided. He felt he was in control of himself again. "Tell me what happened, Mary."

He noticed she was nervously looking at her watch.

Mary closed her eyes as if she were resigning herself to something and said, " I got a call from Carol at about eight this morning. She had gone to Roger's place to pick up some stuff . . ."

"Stuff? What kind of stuff?"

"Stuff. You know — cocaine."

"What the hell are you talking about, Mary? Are you trying to tell me Roger was a dealer?"

"You mean you didn't know? I thought everyone did."

"Of course I didn't know! You say it like he had a sign on his door — 'Roger Billings, Cocaine and things'."

"Anyway, it's true, Morris. I mean he wasn't a major dealer or anything. He just did it part time to support his writing."

"But Roger never touched the stuff! It doesn't make sense!"

"Back then, you mean. But people change, Morris. I know he was dealing. Carol wasn't the only one who got stuff from him."

It wasn't that Morris was shocked. He had seen too many incomprehensible things happen to people over the years. And he had known quite a few who had filtered into the underground economy when the legal one had shut down for them. People had to eat. But he still couldn't picture Roger dealing dope. Not the very same Roger who was once prepared to die on the streets for the revolution.

"Do they know who shot him?" Morris asked.

Mary looked at him strangely. "Of course they do, Morris. Didn't I tell you?"

"Tell me what?"

"He shot himself. Roger committed suicide."

Morris suddenly bolted upright. "You're crazy, Mary! I saw him only yesterday afternoon. He wasn't suicidal!"

"How do you know, Morris? The ones who actually do it aren't always the same people who tell you they might. Besides, I know he was very depressed lately."

Morris sat down and put his head in his hands. "We're all depressed, Mary."

"Well, he was especially depressed about Philip's murder."

"He was collaborating on an article with him, Mary. They weren't lovers."

"Yes they were, Morris."

That was too much for him. "Damn it, Mary! Next thing I know you'll be telling me he was a drag queen!"

"I don't know about that, Morris. But he did write a note."

"A suicide note?"

"Yes. It said, 'Now that my dear Philip is dead I can no longer go on,' or something of that sort."

Morris got up and started pacing the floor. "Mary, did you see the note?"

"No. Carol read it to me over the telephone. She cleaned the house before she called the cops. Now they have it."

"Did she say whether it was handwritten?"

"She found it in his typewriter, so I suppose it was typed."

"Mary, you knew him a long time. Did you ever suspect Roger was gay?"

"Frankly, it shocked the hell out of me. But stranger things have happened."

"Do you know anything about the article he was writing with Philip?"

"Not much. I know it had something to do with drugs and the CIA, though."

He looked at her, trying to catch her eye. "Did you know that Koba was back in town?"

"Koba?"

129

"Yeah. Do you remember him, Mary?"

"Only that he once saved my life."

Morris gave her a curious look. "Tell me about it," he said.

Mary shrugged her shoulders. "It was during the first Stop the Draft Week." She paused to laugh. "Remember that one, Morris?"

"Go on," he said impatiently.

"Well, we were all pressed together outside the Oakland Army Induction Center, trying to block the doors, when suddenly this guy with a bullhorn shouts down from a hotel window across the way that they needed more people up front . . ."

"Gipstein," muttered Morris.

"What?"

"That was Rod Gipstein. He was at an observation post on the fourth floor of the hotel. I remember yelling back to him to come down and join the people."

"Yeah — well, anyway, like the young impetuous kid that I was, I hear the words that bodies are needed up front so, of course, Mary goes. And sure enough, that's when the cops started clubbing. Anyway, there was a mad crush of people starting to retreat. I turned and yelled for them to come back. And when I turned around again, I saw the meanest, ugliest-looking pig I ever laid eyes on. I mean, this cop was a monster. And he had his billy club cocked back like a butcher who's about to kill a turkey . . ." Suddenly Mary's voice began to fade away.

"Shit, Mary! Don't leave me dangling! What happened?"

"Oh, I'm sorry, Morris. You know, I almost died and I was too stupid to understand. That's scary, Morris. That's really scary!"

"So where does Koba come in?"

"Right where the cop's billy club came down. He threw himself between me and the pig and, Christ, was that cop mad! He sure took it out on the poor guy. He beat him senseless."

"Didn't anyone help him?"

"It was pure panic. I tried, but what could I do? They dragged him away. I don't know what happened to him after that. As far as I knew he was dead. Except he never turned up on any list of injured or arrested. Then he appeared again, just

130

before the Strike. He had a jagged scar running down from his scalp to his forehead." She stopped for a moment. She seemed to have drifted back into her memories. Then she looked up at Morris. "When I saw him again, he pretended not to remember me. You know, I never really got a chance to thank him . . ."

Morris had his head bent over. He was thinking. Finally he looked up at Mary and asked, "Do you have any sources downtown anymore?"

"There's always Ronnie Pratt," she said. "Remember him?"

"No," said Morris.

"Well, he was at State College back then. He works in the Police Records Department now."

"Do you have his number?"

"Yeah," said Mary, going over to her Rollidex file. "But he made me promise not to give it out to anyone. He doesn't want people calling him at work."

"Can you call him for me?"

"Why?"

"It's important, Mary."

She looked down at her watch and sighed. "All right, Morris. Then I really do have to go out."

She went into the other room to call. When she came back, she said, "He'll meet you for lunch."

"Where and when?"

"Blanches — at China Basin. Around one. You know where it is?"

"Yeah and it's too expensive," Morris grumbled.

She grabbed her purse and headed for the door. "Fix yourself another cheese sandwich if you like."

Morris walked back to his office with heavy steps. He had given Jack Chesterton the address of a comrade, a friend, and now that man was dead. But if Jack were involved, what would have been his motive? And why would he have been so obvious? Certainly an experienced CIA operative could have done the job cleanly without making himself a prime suspect.

So that left Koba. Rocky said Koba was dead. Jack said he was

131

alive. Chances were, he thought to himself, Jack was on the level. He was just too late, that's all.

The Meat Market was filled with the late-morning crowd when Morris came in. Larry was hurriedly making a bunch of ham-on-ryes.

"Any messages for me?" asked Morris.

"Some chick called about a divorce. I told her you don't do 'em."

"Only if I get desperate," said Morris.

"That's not what it says on your card," Larry replied, looking up and putting the mustard knife in the jam by accident.

"You've got my card done?" asked Morris.

"Not yet," said Larry. "It's almost on the drawing board, though."

Morris went back to the walk-in fridge and found a seat. He took the casebook out of his jacket pocket and wrote a few more things down. He ended by tracing some squiggles and then tapping his pencil contemplatively on the table.

There were twists and turns which seemed to be going off into space. But everything led somewhere, he thought to himself. It might not be visible to the naked eye, but they led somewhere.

What if everything that was reported back to him was true? What if Philip really was shot by a madman and Roger had committed suicide? What if Philip and Roger really were lovers? Certainly Mary had no trouble in believing it. Nor, he supposed, would Heather. Fredo didn't believe anything. For him it was just another elaborate game of murder most foul.

But what about the old lady in front of La Bohème. Could she have been the victim of a random bullet, too? He scribbled some words on his sheet of paper. "If truth is madness then madness is truth." He tapped his pencil again. What turned coincidence, no matter how striking, into conspiracy? The Left was so immersed in martyrdom that it didn't take a giant leap of imagination to believe their enemies were capable of anything — even murder. But what about Latin America? What of those countries where hundreds of bodies turn up every day, bloated in some ditch, shroud white and stinking of putrefaction? No one disbelieved that the governments there were responsible. So we were supposedly a democracy, he thought. So the leaders here supposedly believed in repressive tolerance, as Marcuse had said. But what was Latin America anyway, if not an extension of the Mission District? The borders were just fabricated to restrict the flow of capital and to make it easier for rich people to survive. Borders weren't created by working people. They didn't give a shit about borders. Borders were just another way of keeping them in line. Terror was another. Maybe terror was less appropriate in the United States. That didn't mean they wouldn't use it. It just meant they'd use it more judiciously. Maybe they didn't want blood in the streets. Maybe just a few dead bodies were enough to temper the quirk for justice. A few dead bodies to make you think about the consequences, to give you a different perspective.

"A few dead bodies . . ." he said aloud.

A young woman at the next table looked up from her book and decided to move into the other room.

Suddenly he realized he had to get in touch with Heather. He had to warn her about what was going on. But where could he phone her? She was working at Hunter's Point, she had said. But what school?

He went over to the phone booth and looked up the number for the school board. He dialed and asked to be connected with the substitutes office. He told the woman who answered that it was an emergency. It took her a while to look up Heather's assignment, but, in the end, she found it and gave him a number to call. He hung up and dialed again.

The school secretary was very surprised. "You say you're her husband? But she phoned in sick today!"

"She did? I'm sorry, I'm calling from out of town."

"Well phone your house," she suggested.

He telephoned Heather at her flat. There was no response.

He rubbed his head and then phoned Fredo. Fredo was home. Fredo was always home.

"Can you come over to the office?" Morris asked.

"Now?"

"Yeah, now."

"Is it important?"

"Very!"

Morris had just finished his second cappuccino when Fredo arrived. "Can you lend me some dough?" he said.

"You brought me all the way over here to borrow some dough?" asked Fredo, looking at him with ill-disguised frustration.

"No. I want to talk to you about something. But I also need to borrow some dough."

Fredo got out his wallet and handed him a ten-dollar bill.

"Thanks," he said.

"If I got it, you're welcome to it," said Fredo. "If I'm short, I'll come to you."

Morris got up and ordered some drinks from Larry. He used the change to buy himself a pack of smokes.

"What's up?" asked Fredo when Morris returned to the table.

He handed Fredo a cup of espresso and a cigarette. The condemned man deserves that at least, he said to himself. And then, to Fredo, he said, "I think we're in trouble."

Fredo opened his eyes so wide that Morris thought of two full moons spinning, bloodshot, in his head. "What do you mean 'we'? I ain't done nothin' since 1974."

"Neither have I," replied Morris. "But that's not the point."

"What is the point?"

"I'm not sure." Then he realized that Fredo probably didn't know. "Roger's dead. Mary said he committed suicide."

Fredo was silent. Morris looked at him. The information hadn't seemed to register.

"Did you hear me, Fredo?"

Fredo nodded. "Was it drugs?"

"You knew?"

"I knew that Roger was in a bad way. He asked me to lend him some dough about a month ago. But he wanted too much. I don't have that kind of money."

"You knew he was dealing?"

"Sure. Didn't you?"

Morris shook his head. "I hadn't seen him for some time." He was about to add that maybe he'd try to see Roger more often. Then he reminded himself that Roger was dead. It was difficult to accept that death meant a permanent change of status. There were no visiting rights. "I don't think he committed suicide," he said.

"I thought you said he did."

"That's what Mary said. Carol found him this morning when she went to his house. She phoned Mary. She found a note that said Roger killed himself because he couldn't go on living without Philip."

Fredo spat out a mouthful of coffee, spraying it over the table and Morris' clothes. "I'm sorry," he apologised. "I just thought I heard you say that Roger killed himself because he couldn't live without Philip."

"That's what the suicide note said," Morris replied, wiping himself off with a handkerchief.

"Do you believe that?" asked Fredo.

"No. Do you?"

"I don't believe anyone would kill themselves because of Philip. They might kill Philip because of Philip, but not themselves."

"What about the note?"

"An obvious forgery."

"I agree," said Morris. "I think that Roger and Philip were killed by the same person for the same reason."

"Who and what?" asked Fredo, raising his eyebrows in a challenging manner.

"Koba. Because of the article."

"What article?"

"I saw Roger at the wake. He said that he and Philip were collaborating on an article about the drug trade. Somehow Koba was involved."

Fredo lit his cigarette. "It all sounds pretty flimsy," he said, taking in a deep breath of smoke. "You've got nothing to go on except a ten-second phone call and the rumor of an article."

Morris lit up, too, and let the smoke trail from his mouth. "Sure it's flimsy. But I still think it's Koba."

"But why?" asked Fredo. "Just because we once suspected him of being an agent? You've got to give me more than that, Morris. If someone is going to take revenge, there has to be something to be revengeful about. Nobody kills anyone because of an article. They might sue someone, but they don't kill them."

"What if they're about to be exposed?"

"Exposed for what? I might write an article accusing you of trafficking drugs. What would that mean? It would probably just give you more business."

"Then what are you suggesting, Fredo?"

"I don't know. But the most logical answer is that the two killings are unrelated. Most likely, Roger was killed because he was mixed up in the drug trade — a vendetta or something. Philip was killed for something else. You've linked them in your mind because you know them both and because of your own paranoia."

"How about the note, Fredo? Even if it was a forgery, it still links Philip and Roger. Whoever wrote it made the case themselves."

"The person who wrote it might not be the same person who killed him. You didn't see the note. You heard about it third hand. Carol, herself, could have written the note for purposes of her own. Or maybe Mary misunderstood her. Or maybe the person who killed him wanted to make it appear that there was a link."

"This isn't one of your detective books, Fredo. There's other ways of understanding things. One doesn't always need facts."

Fredo shrugged. "Morris, you can believe whatever you want to believe. If you want to convince others, though, you need facts — even if you have to make them up yourself."

"You can trap yourself in facts, too, Fredo. Facts are commodities. They can be bought and sold like peaches or sardines. They can be processed, canned, broadcast, or plastered on walls. They can be conjured up like rabbits from a hat. They can be hidden in shirt sleeves and served up as sandwiches for tea. But they can't convince me Koba didn't bump off Philip Lampam and Roger Billings. That I know."

"Then come up with some facts that prove it, Morris."

"Well, I hope to come up with an explanation, Fredo. And I hope to do it soon — before it's too late."

"Too late for what?" he asked.

"Too late to save your bloody neck!" said Morris, getting up from his chair and stomping out.

Chapter Eleven

He used an ancient transfer from his collection and caught a bus to China Basin. It was early when he arrived so he walked along the Bay, reacquainting himself with the area. He hadn't worked these docks much in his longshore days. When Redwood City was still a forest the waters here had been alive with barges filled with lumber and tar. Then came the heavy industry that kept it busy through World War II. But now it was quiet; the warehouses had become offices and cafés and showplaces for the rich. The great steel cranes lay idle.

Blanches was crowded when he arrived. But the pier was nearly deserted due to the damp chill in the air. Of the three men braving the wind, only two seemed to fit the bill. The other was too old and paunchy. One looked vaguely familiar. Morris sat down beside him.

"Ronnie Pratt?"

The man gave him a strange look.

A voice from the other side of the pier called out, "You're looking for me, Morris."

Morris turned around. It was the paunchy one.

"You don't remember me?" he asked as Morris walked over to him.

"How could I forget?" said Morris offering his hand. Up close the man didn't look so old. Morris supposed it was the grey hair and flab that made him appear to be upward in years. In fact, he might have been the same age as Morris. That thought made him cringe. He wondered what he, himself, looked like at a distance. Perhaps people wrote him off as an ancient relic — the sort nomadic tribes would leave behind when the weather grew harsh enough to move on.

Pratt was eating a crab salad, piled high with avocado and

covered with a thick layer of dressing. Morris took out the sandwich he had made at Mary's. "They don't mind, do you think?" He motioned toward the restaurant.

He shook his head. "Not if you're sitting with me. It would be different if you came here alone." He took an enormous forkful of crab, dripping in Louie sauce, and stuffed it in his mouth. Morris watched in quiet wonder.

"What did you want to see me about?" Pratt asked, wiping his lips with the paper napkin Blanche had thoughtfully provided.

"I need some information on two killings — one that happened about a week ago; the other one, last night."

"Are you a reporter now?"

Morris shook his head. "I'm an investigator."

"You're interested in Roger Billings and Philip Lampam, Mary said."

Morris nodded. "Did you know them?"

"Only casually. It would have been hard not to have known them, though. They both had pretty big mouths." He stuffed some more crab salad into his own mouth and chewed. Morris thought of a cow and its cud.

"So what's the connection, other than the obvious one that both of them were in SDS?" Pratt continued.

"Don't you find it suspicious that they were both shot so close in time — just several days apart?"

Pratt wiped the dressing that had begun to dribble down his chin. "Suspicious, no. Curious, yes. Besides, Mary said Roger's death was suicide." He pointed to Morris' sandwich. "Aren't you hungry?"

Morris thought it almost obscene that Pratt was fishing for his sandwich after such a caloric lunch. He took a proprietary bite. Pratt looked somewhat disappointed.

"I'd like to see the police files on both of them. Is that possible?"

The wind was starting to blow in from the bay. It had a sting to it. Morris pulled his jacket tighter. The buttons were missing so he had to hold it closed.

"Are you cold?" Pratt asked. "Do you want to go inside for some dessert?"

138

Morris shook his head. It had been sunny that morning in Noe Valley, but down here by the Bay his lips were turning blue.

Pratt gave him a strange look. "You're shivering, you know. Why don't you button your jacket at least?"

"Can you get the records for me?" asked Morris.

"Maybe," he said. "But why do you want to know?"

In the distance a container ship began to wind its way through their end of the Bay. A flock of seagulls hovered overhead. Morris wondered what garbage was being thrown overboard that made the seagulls hover around. What had the seamen eaten for lunch? Hash? Baked beans? Crab Louie?

"Why do you want to know?" Pratt asked again.

Suddenly he saw him anew. The rounds of fat seemed to be melting from his face like wax underneath a match. As the fat melted, a new face was born. It was more recognizable and Morris remembered.

"Why do you want to know?" It was 1968. He was standing next to the student cafeteria. The man in front was staring at him with a fixed gaze.

"You're one of the leaders, aren't you? Why are you holding back?" It was Pratt. He was thin. His voice was insistent.

"I'm not holding back," Morris replied. What did he mean by "one of the leaders", anyway? Was it because Morris spoke up at meetings? And wasn't that what SDS was all about — participatory democracy? Just because some of them didn't participate was no reason to make leaders out of those who did.

"What did you want to ask me?" Morris had said. "I'm in a hurry!"

"I wanted to know the position of the Black Student Union on Albania. Do they support Enver Hoxha?"

Morris had felt his blood boil. "Why the hell do you want to know that?"

"It's important to me."

"Well, go ask them yourself!"

It was his eyes that gave it away. The face was fatter. The body more grotesque. But the eyes were the same.

"I want to find out if there's any connection beween their

deaths." said Morris. "For example, if the bullets that killed them were fired from the same gun."

"I see."

"It's important to me."

Pratt was searching around for some crumbs of food to eat. He licked his finger and moved it over his empty plate like a vacuum cleaner.

"Will you do it?"

Pratt smiled. "Have Mary call me tomorrow."

Morris stood up. "How about if I call?"

"Have Mary call."

Morris nodded and started to walk off. Then he stopped and turned. "Say, can I borrow a dime?"

Pratt looked up at him incredulously. "A dime?"

"Yes. I have to make a phone call."

"Will you pay me back?"

"Of course."

Pratt stuck a fat hand into a pocket and retrieved a thin, silvery coin. He looked at it and handed it, reluctantly, to Morris.

He tried phoning Rocky, but he couldn't get through. He ended up deciding to chance it and took a bus to Rocky's office.

Rocky's secretary was not impressed by Morris' protestation when he arrived and demanded entry to the inner sanctum. Morris had come without an appointment and, she said, he would have to wait.

"It's a matter of life and death," he said.

"I'm not trying to put you off, Mr Kaplan," the secretary replied, "but I have heard that one before. He's with an important client. I really don't know whether he'll be able to see you today at all."

There are two types of barriers, thought Morris. One is physical and the other psychological. Both are meant to keep you out. He was determined to get in.

So he waited fifteen minutes or so and then, hearing laughter from within the oaken door, he stood up and boldly walked past the guardian of the gates.

"You can't go in there, Mr Kaplan!" she shouted.

"'Cant' is just another word for pious platitude," he said, barging his way inside.

Rocky was passing a joint to a bald man dressed in a rayon suit, who looked like one of the seedy characters Morris had noticed hanging around the Broadway strip joints.

"I'm sorry, Mr Calhoon, he just ran right past . . ." The secretary stood at the door, pale and trembling.

"What do you want, Morris?" asked Rocky, standing up and glaring at him. He was obviously not amused.

"Roger's dead," said Morris, getting directly to the point. "I think you know why."

The bald man stood up too. "What's going on, Calhoon? I thought this was my appointment." He looked anxiously at his watch.

"It is Bruno. Don't worry about it, OK?" Turning to Morris, he said, "You don't know what you're talking about. But whatever you have to say can wait. I'm busy right now."

"Roger said you have a copy of his article. I want to see it."

"What's this guy want from you, Calhoon? I think I should fatten his lip!" The bald man looked at Rocky for a sign of agreement.

Morris sat down in a chair beside the heavy shelves filled with dusty law books. "I'm not leaving till you show it to me, Rocky," he said firmly.

Rocky covered his face with his hand. "Please, Morris, not a sit-in! Not today!"

"You want me to break his arm, Calhoon?" asked the bald man, taking a few steps toward Morris.

"Let me handle this, Bruno," said Rocky with a note of annoyance. He looked at Morris and said, "Koba's dead. If you know what's good for you, you'll leave now without waiting to be asked again."

Morris shook his head. "Give me the article," he said stubbornly.

Rocky walked over to the chair where Morris was sitting. "Help me carry him out of here, Bruno."

"Sure thing, Calhoon," said the bald man, with an ugly grin on his pasty face. And each of them grabbed an arm of the chair,

141

carrying it and Morris into the waiting-room. Then, dropping it like a concrete weight into a muddy lake, they went back into Rocky's chamber, slamming the big oak door behind them.

"Your old man would be ashamed of you, Rocky!" Morris called after him.

"Get out of here, Kaplan!" a voice shouted back.

"If you change your mind, you can reach me at my office," Morris yelled through the keyhole.

"Leave your card with my secretary!" an angry voice replied from within.

"He wanted me to leave my card with you," said Morris to Rocky's secretary who was glaring at him with daggers in her eyes, "but I seem to be all out. So if you lend me a pen . . ."

She continued to glare.

"Never mind," he said, "I've got one." And he took a bit of paper from his otherwise empty wallet and wrote, "Morris Kaplan, Public Eye. Meat Market Café. No Job Too Big Or Small. No Divorces." Then he put it down on her desk.

"You might want to start a file," he suggested.

She continued to glare.

"Bye." He wiggled a finger at her. Then he walked away.

He took a bus back to Noe Valley and got off at 23rd Street. He walked till he reached Roger's address.

Standing outside the lonely cottage door, he tried to summon up the courage to go inside. He had never done this sort of thing before — entering a dead writer's study, uninvited and unannounced. It was, to his mind, worse than desecrating a grave. But he felt certain that whatever chance there was to solve this mystery lay in the research that Roger and Philip had done before they departed.

A chill breeze blew down from Diamond Heights. Above, the shrouds of mist descended, soon to cover the entire city with a blanket of grey. He pulled up the collar of his jacket and, taking a deep breath, tried to turn the handle of the door. To his surprise (and dismay) it opened.

Roger had lived alone in this rear cottage off Noe and 23rd. To reach it one had to go down a back alleyway and through a neighboring garden. It was secluded and, perhaps, that was why no one heard the gunshot whenever it occurred. Or maybe they just didn't care. A gunshot or a firecracker, a car backfiring on the empty streets, they all sounded the same. And who would dare to investigate at that hour in the morning?

The eerie part, however, was how similar the place was to the one where Morris lived. There were a number of these little cottages in back gardens in this area. They all had lonely tenants who could easily be shot and left to die without a hope of being discovered.

Morris walked inside. The front room was uncharacteristically clean. Carol had done a good job straightening for the dead. Roger had never kept it so orderly when he was alive. Morris wondered whether he would have been pleased or annoyed at the unwarranted intrusion. The dead are so powerless over those kind of things, he thought. When he died they'd finally get a chance to cut his hair, shave his beard and dress him in a clean suit, just as they had always wanted. And he wouldn't be able to do a damn thing about it.

Roger's study was off to the side, in a little alcove. There was a desk with an old-fashioned typewriter (probably the one that was used to type the suicide note), a file cabinet, and several cardboard boxes filled with unsorted clippings.

Morris went directly to the file cabinet, opened the metal drawer and began to leaf through the dividers. It didn't take long to find the one he wanted. It was a folder marked with big red letters: "KOBA". He pulled it from the drawer and opened it up. It was empty.

"Looking for something, Kaplan?" It was an ugly voice. The kind that sends chills down blackboards.

Morris felt the floor open up underneath his feet. If there had been any man-eating crocodiles below, he probably would have preferred them to what he was about to face.

He turned around. It was Lieutenant Brian Murphy with his dog, a cop who looked as if he ate pussycats like Morris for breakfast along with his bowl of nails.

Morris smiled as charmingly as he knew how. "Hello, Murphy," he said. "Nice to see you again."

"Taken to grave robbing now, huh, Kaplan? That's what's so nice about you commie queers. Not only do you bump yourselves off, saving us the trouble, but you also come back to the scene of the crime so we don't even have to go out to get you."

"I was — uh — looking for some papers I'd left here," Morris said.

"Poison-pen letters?" Murphy walked over to where Morris was standing by the desk and picked up the folder. "Or this file?"

"Whatever was inside was missing," said Morris.

"Maybe it never existed," said Murphy with a nasty smile.

"It existed," said Morris. "The question is, who took it?"

Murphy looked at his dog. "Did you take anything, Sergeant Crowley? I think this commie creep just accused you of theft."

"I don't like that," said Crowley, coming up to Morris. "You should respect us policemen 'cause we're here to protect you." And with one swift movement he punched Morris in the belly.

Morris doubled over in pain. "That wasn't necessary, you neurotic hyena," he groaned.

"Just like old times, Kaplan. I bet you missed calling us names."

"Yeah, I go to the zoo twice a week to let it all out."

Crowley sent his fist flying toward Morris' solar plexus.

Morris gasped for air. "Tell your baboon to lay off, Murphy! It's bad enough that Koba's trying to get us, without your ape doing his soft-shoe routine!"

"Koba?" said Murphy. "I thought he was one of yours. Well, I wish him luck. Say 'goodbye' to the gentleman, Crowley."

Crowley shoved his elbow into Morris' kidney, smashing him up against the desk. Morris crumpled to the ground.

"Go ahead and take what you want, Kaplan. I don't think your friend would mind." And saying that, the two cops walked out the door, leaving it open behind them. Through the gap the fog seeped in.

Morris dragged himself back to his cottage. He surprised himself at still being able to walk. But nothing had been broken except, possibly, his pride. And pride wasn't much of a commodity these days; it wasn't even listed on the stock exchange.

144

In the garden, Arnold was marching like a toy soldier, back and forth along the rows of plants, his shotgun balanced on his shoulder.

"Guarding the crops against field mice, Arnold?" Morris said, resting his aching body against the garden gate.

"Field mice and other things," said Arnold. "Someone's been at my vegetables again."

"It's not worth a murder rap," said Morris.

Arnold put his rifle at parade rest. "Protecting your property and loved ones is written into our constitution, Morris." Looking closer at the disheveled figure holding onto the gate, he said, "I'm glad to see you've taken my advice and finally started doing some exercising."

"Yeah, I've been throwing myself against brick walls and rolling in rusty nails."

"Well, that's up to you," said Arnold. "But it is good to get the old heart pumping again, isn't it?"

"It certainly is, Arnold," he said, struggling to get his body into motion. He made it to the stairs and then turning back around he said, "Hey, is that thing loaded?" He pointed to Arnold's shotgun.

"Of course, Morris! You don't think I'm doing this for fun, do you?"

"I'm not sure what anyone does for kicks anymore," said Morris under his breath as he made his way up to the cottage door.

Inside it was quiet and dark. He slipped off his shoes and lay his aching body down in bed. In a few moments he was fast asleep.

The tapping sound was persistent enough to rouse him from his dream. He sat up in bed and rubbed his eyes.

"Who's there?" he shouted.

There was no reply. Just more flurries of taps.

Grumbling, he got out of bed, somewhat surprised that he was still fully clothed, and peeked through the window. It was Rosa, looking for all the world like a pup who had been tossed over the side of a bridge on a dark and stormy night. Except that it was still day.

"Rosa!" he said, opening the door. "What are you doing here?"

She looked past him, through the open door. "Can I come in?"

145

"Sure, Rosa . . ." He needn't have said it. She was already pushing herself inside. "What are you doing here? How come you're not home?"

"Can't I even come visit my own pa?" she asked, looking at him with cow-like eyes.

"Sure, but . . ."

"I runned away," she said flatly.

"You ran away?" It was then he noticed the little rucksack she had slung over her shoulder. "Why?"

She sat down on his bed with a bounce. "I don't wanna go to Chicago!"

"Oh, so that's it . . ." He stopped for an instant and then he asked, "Heather decided to move there? She told you so?"

"She didn't have to tell me. I heard her talking to that guy." She made a face of intense dislike.

"I see."

"So I decided to come live with you."

"Live with me?"

"Sure!" She threw him one of her most charming smiles. "We could start a father and daughter detective agency! I could help you with your case! We can be roommates — just like the old days!"

"Uh . . . yeah, Rosa. But, you know, this place isn't very big . . ."

"I'm not very big either," she said. "Honest, I wouldn't get in the way."

"Where would you sleep?"

"We could build me one of those bunk beds in the corner over here. Remember the one you built for me when I was a little kid?" She obviously had the whole thing worked out.

"I remember."

"So?"

"It's just not that simple."

Tears started forming in her eyes. "It's real simple, Moishe. Either you want me or you don't. Make up your mind."

"Sure I want you, Rosa . . ."

The bright smile was back on her face. "It's settled then!" She started looking around the room. "I could help you fix this place

146

up. It sure could use some brightness!" She walked over to the mantelpiece. "I like these flowers! We could put more of them around the room!" She looked at the card which was still tied to the bouquet with a bright red ribbon and read it aloud. "'Darling, I love Puccini as much as you. See you soon. Yours forever, Bubbles.'"

She giggled. "Who's Bubbles, Moishe?"

He shrugged. "You got me."

"You mean you don't know? Who sent 'em to you? Maybe it's a code, Moishe! You think?"

"Maybe."

"What's a Puccini?"

"An Italian composer. He wrote operas . . ." Suddenly Morris stopped and rubbed his cheek.

"Does that mean something, Moishe?"

"I don't know."

"Hey, I got an idea!" she said, coming over and bouncing down on his bed again. "Let's celebrate!"

"Celebrate?"

"Yeah! Let's have a celebration — now that we're back together again!" Her eyes were sparkling. "I know! Let's go to Chinatown and have a pork bun! Just like we used to do!"

"You mean at that dim sum place on Pacific Avenue?"

"Yeah! That one!"

Maybe that was the way to break it to her, he thought. Over a pork bun in Chinatown. "OK," he said. "Put on your hat, grab your stuff and let's go."

They took the "J" trolly and transferred to the Stockton bus. They got off at the edge of Chinatown and wandered through that fragrant maze of alleyways where East met West in bright, exotic façades and West met East behind closed doors of squalid rooms and cruel sweatshops.

But outside, on the main streets where wide-eyed tourists wandered without much comprehension, the shops had the nature of a magnificent Oriental bazaar. And such wonderful things were displayed: splendid fish from distant Pacific waters and other curious creatures from the sea, live and splashing in aquarium tanks; featherless ducks and geese garroted and still hanging by the neck to dry; little Chinese cookies in infinite shapes, piled high, colorfully painted; strange herbs and spices for preserving or healing or increasing sexual delights; ginseng roots in water-filled flasks, floating like embryos in an anatomy laboratory; acupuncture clinics with golden needle signs; and dark, inscrutable restaurants with forbidding entrances and food that was delectably fine.

"I like it here," said Rosa, tugging on her cap to stop it from blowing away. "I like getting lost in the crowds. Remember when we used to go to the park?" She pointed to an area at the bottom of Washington Street where old men were doing t'ai chi exercises and playing mah-jong games. "You used to swing me there with all the little Chinese kids. Remember?"

He remembered all right.

"Thems were the good old days, huh, Moishe?"

"Thems were the good old days," he replied.

They made their way through the crowded streets to their favorite dim sum shop on Pacific Avenue. As usual it was jammed with people ordering dinners to go.

"Listen, Rosa," he said, as they stood in the take-away line, "about your coming to live with me . . ."

"I thought that was all settled, Moishe," she said. He heard the disappointment in her voice.

"Don't you think we ought to bring Heather in on the decision, though?"

"Is Heather asking you whether she should go to Chicago?"

"No . . ."

She turned so he couldn't see her face. "I don't think you want me to stay with you."

He sighed. "All right, let's discuss it after we eat our pork buns."

"Yeah. I'll wait for you outside," she said in a tearful voice as she headed toward the door.

It took him another ten minutes to make his way to the front of the line. He ordered some pork buns and, as an added treat, some shrimp cakes. The whole thing came to less than a buck and a half.

He pushed his way through the mass of waiting customers to the door. Outside the traffic was backed up all the way to Grant Street. Horns were blaring; the discordant sounds were punctuated by angry shouts. He stood on the pavement looking up the hill and then down as people hurriedly shoved by.

"Rosa!" he called out. And he muttered to himself, "Where the hell is that kid?" For, indeed, she was nowhere to be seen.

It was late in the evening when he dragged himself into the Meat Market Café. For the last few hours, besides trying to call Heather at every available pay-phone, he had searched the underbelly of San Francisco — anywhere he thought a street kid might hang out. It was a heart-rending journey which took him from the rinky-tink dives of Broadway to the dingy pinball palaces on Market Street and, finally, the depressing alleyways of Polk Street where young bodies were bought and sold like bags of rice. Yet even someone like him, who thought he knew San Francisco inside out, could hardly believe the number of homeless children he found, drugged or drunk or on the make or just simply walking the streets spaced out of their ever-loving minds.

A relief man was on duty at the Meat Market that night. Someone he didn't know.

"My name's Kaplan — Morris Kaplan," he said, going up to the counter. "Were there any messages for me?"

"Kaplan?" said the guy. He put a finger to his chin and tapped. "Seems to me there was . . ."

"Well look, will you?" Morris said in an abrupt tone of voice.

"I didn't write it down," said the counter man. "But it was from a woman. She said something about taking a ride someplace . . ."

"Someplace?"

"Yeah, someplace like the Valley of the Moon — someplace like that . . ."

"She say anything about my kid? Her name's Rosa."

"Yeah, I think she did."

"Well what the hell did she say?" Morris nearly shouted.

The counter man gave him a strange look. "I think she said

she's staying with a friend." And then, as an afterthought, the guy said, "You get a lot of calls here? Is this your office, buddy?"

"Yes, you dumb schmuck," said Morris, turning to leave, "as a matter of fact it is!"

Chapter Twelve

He stumbled into the Meat Market early the next morning, raw and bleary-eyed — the aftermaths of a miserable night of sweats and shakes and disconnected phone lines. Larry was behind the counter drawing a picture of a customer being devoured by a pack of hungry wolves.

"Any messages?" asked Morris in a gravelly voice.

"Yeah," said Larry, pulling out his notebook. "Two. Big day for you, huh?"

"Big day," Morris agreed. "I'll have a double espresso, OK?"

Larry did a quick sketch of a steaming drink on his pad and handed it to him.

"No jokes today," he said. "I'm not in the mood."

"You're never in the mood anymore, Morris. In fact, you're no fun at all lately."

"You're dealing with a bruised psyche, Larry. Do me a favor and cut the clowning. I need a double espresso and some change for the phone."

He made the coffee and handed him the change. "How does Heather stand you?" he asked.

"The simple answer is that she doesn't."

"What's the complicated answer?"

Morris gave him a look and then retreated to his office. He opened his messages. One was from Heather. It read: "Tried calling you at home, but your phone is out of order. Jeff and I took a ride down to Half Moon Bay. Rosa's staying with a friend. Give me a ring sometime this evening." The other was from Rocky. It read: "If you want to talk, I'll be at the Hyatt Regency this afternoon. The lower bar at four."

He drank his coffee and pondered his situation. Heather was somewhere with that creep, Jeffery. Rosa was with a friend,

151

location unknown. Fredo didn't want to get involved. And the rest of them were too caught up in their own lives to give him a second thought. So who else was there? The police? He could just imagine himself trying to convince Lieutenant Murphy to bail him out. Then there was Jack, of course. But he couldn't even contact him.

He took out his casebook and glanced through it. There was just one thing left to do: keep plodding on. He made a notation: "Meet Rocky — Hyatt, 4pm. Before that, get in touch with Mary. Have her phone Ronnie Pratt to see if he has any info on Philip and Roger's deaths for me."

Draining the last drops of his espresso, he closed his casebook, stuck it in his pocket, and got up to leave.

"Tough times, I guess," said Larry, catching Morris' expression as he walked past.

"You can say that again," Morris replied.

"Times are changing," said Larry. "It just ain't what it was. Take the Meat Market for instance. It used to be that people liked this sort of place — scuzzy but nice; somewhere you could feel comfortable enough to hang your hat. But not anymore. Now they want polished tables and fancy goods. Everyone's going up-market, Morris."

"Everyone except me," said Morris.

"There's still a few of us around," said Larry. "Just not enough to pay the bills."

He took a walk up Castro Street and down the other side of the hill. He stopped at an outdoor telephone booth and gave a call to Mary.

"Can I come over?" he asked.

"It's not terribly convenient, Morris."

"Come on, Mary. It's important."

"So is what I'm doing."

"I need your help."

She let out a sigh. "All right. Come over in an hour."

Mary was an enigma to him. He had known her since '67 and he still felt she was a mystery. He had always wondered about her link to the movement, coming from a small country town steeped in Protestant evangelism while all the rest of them had come from the urban middle class. She had never expressed her feelings in a passionate way. But she was great at busy work. She was dependable. And she was always there to lean on, like a comfortable lamppost.

Other people had gone their own way. They had disconnected while she kept trying to keep things together, like piling sandbags on a flood-battered dike. Why had she tried so hard? Did she think she could resurrect the '60s? But Mary was OK. A real friend in time of need. He supposed he had been unfair thinking of her in that way. Maybe he resented being put off.

He found himself on the corner of Castro and Market. Turning right on Market, he continued down the street where all the "tchachka" shops stood in a row. He wondered who bought all that junk. Not that some of it wasn't funny. But the thought of people making a living by selling wind-up plastic teeth, nose rings, and electric penises, seemed to defy logic. Yet who was he to complain? He had never bought anything in his life that couldn't be smoked, read, eaten, drunk or worn without ironing. If the economy had to depend on him, it was in serious trouble.

He stopped by the Café Flore. Ordering some coffee, he found a place to sit outside. He glanced over at the people at the next table and wondered what possessed them to paint their bodies in such a tribal way. Then he caught himself. Could it be that ultra-violet hair wasn't that much different from a "stop-the-war" button? Then again, he thought, maybe it was.

He sat for a while and finally, looking at his watch, he got up and started walking back toward Noe Hill. He arrived at Mary's place about an hour after he had phoned her.

Mary took a long time answering his persistent knocking at her door. When at last she came, he could hardly recognize her. She was beaming. It was as if someone had transformed her into a cherub. Her face was pink and her eyes sparkled. She wore a blissful smile. Morris wondered whether she had suffered a religious revelation. What did they call it now? Born again? As if once wasn't enough!

"Hello, Morris. Come in! I'm leaving in a minute, but come in

153

anyway." She motioned with her hand as if she were inviting him into a fairy tale.

"You look different, Mary. Are you on something?"

"Oh, Morris, Morris, Morris! You wouldn't understand. I'm in love!"

"That's nice," he said. He looked around. There were several suitcases piled by the landing. "Are you going on a trip?"

She giggled like a schoolgirl. "I'm getting married, Morris. Imagine that!"

He couldn't. "Who's the lucky guy?" he asked.

The laughter trilled from her lips. Her voice was an octave higher than usual. "What a silly man you are! Where have you been? Oh, never mind! You'll always be Morris, won't you? I mean, you can't change! Not like the rest of us . . ." There were tears in her eyes as her words gushed out.

"Are you OK, Mary?" he asked, looking at her curiously.

"OK? Me? I'm euphoric!"

A buxom young woman walked down the stairs. "Are you ready, Honeybear?" she asked.

Morris turned around. "Hi, Carol," he said.

Carol glanced at him and nodded. Then she looked back at Mary. "The plane leaves in an hour, babe. We got to get our ass in gear."

"Right away, Pussycat." She turned to Morris. "Isn't it thrilling? South America! We're going to sail down the Amazon into the jungle." She threw her arms around Morris and gave him a kiss. "Goodbye," she said.

"What about Pratt? You were supposed to call him for me . . ."

"Call him yourself," she said, grabbing one of the suitcases and following "Pussycat" outside. She handed him the key to the door as she passed. "Just put it through the mail slot when you're done. Maybe I'll see you in a month. Maybe never."

He watched her go. Then he rubbed his head and went over to her desk to search through her Rollidex file. He found Pratt's office number and copied it down.

"I thought I told you to have Mary call," Pratt said when Morris finally got through to him.

"Mary left for the Amazon with her fiancée," Morris replied. There was a silence on the other end.

"Hello?" He wondered whether Pratt had hung up on him.

"I was afraid that was going to happen," Pratt said finally. "Now what am I going to do?"

"About what?"

"I loved her, Morris. I loved her . . ."

"Christ!" Morris thought to himself. "Has the whole world gone mad?"

"Do you know what it is to really love someone, Morris? To be obsessed with her night and day? To dream about her when you're sleeping and when you're eating? Do you know what that feels like, Morris?"

He didn't know whether Pratt wanted a response or not. He couldn't imagine him dreaming of anything besides food. Maybe Pratt pictured Mary as a custard pudding or a mutton chop.

"Ronnie," he said, "I hate to ask you at a time like this, but did you get the information I needed?"

"What a callous question, Morris. Don't you have a spark of human decency?"

"I'm sorry Mary ran out on you, Ronnie. Truly I am. But I'm trying to save some lives right now and I need that information. Couldn't you give it to me?"

"You want to know? Well, fuck you then! The records are missing, Morris! They're gone!"

"What do you mean?"

"I mean they're gone! Wiped off the computer! They've vanished from the face of the earth!"

He felt the ache in his head grow increasingly more painful as he walked back to his cottage. When he got there, he went straight to the bathroom and filled the washbasin with cold water. Then he bent down and immersed his head. For half a second he thought of just leaving it there. But the idea of drowning himself like that seemed too ludicrous even for him.

Eventually he straightened up and shook himself like a mangy dog who had managed to fall into a polluted lake. He looked in

155

the mirror above the sink and decided he didn't much like what he saw.

There was a crackling noise in his ears as he dried himself off. At first he thought it might have been a build-up of wax, but after cleaning each ear with a cotton swab, he realized the noise was coming from outside his head. He listened more closely. It sounded very much like static.

He went into the other room and checked his radio. It was turned off. To make certain, he pulled out the plug. But the noise continued unabated.

"I wonder if static can come out of your brain?" he asked aloud.

Then he located it — the noise was emanating from someplace over by the mantelpiece. He went over to that side of the room and suddenly he understood — it was coming from the flowers!

"What the hell is this?" he said.

"Hello?" A metallic voice came through.

"Hello?" Morris answered back.

"Morris?"

"Is that you, Jack?"

"Where are you standing?"

"Right by the mantelpiece."

"Well, move back a foot or two. Sit down in a chair or on the bed. You don't have to be so close. The mike is quite sensitive."

Jack's voice sounded tinny, as if it were coming from an old-fashioned radio set. Morris debated for a moment whether to chuck the flowers immediately into the toilet. He wondered what a flush would sound like at Jack's end.

"Are you still there, Morris?"

"Yes, I'm still here. What do you want before I plant you in the garden?"

"Morris, you're in trouble. Big trouble."

Morris gritted his teeth. "Look, why don't we cut out all the bull. Why did you tell me that you left the CIA when you obviously haven't?"

"Trust me, Morris. I'm on your side."

Morris threw his hands in the air and looked away from the flowers. "Trust you? Are you mad or am I?"

There was a momentary silence. "I can still help you . . ."

"Like you helped Roger?" Morris shot back.

"Calm down," said the voice. "Why don't you fix yourself a drink?"

"You drank all the whisky, remember?"

"All right," said the voice, "just settle down."

Morris sat down on a chair, facing the mantelpiece. He rubbed his head. "What did you find out, Jack?"

"How much do you know, Morris?"

"I went to Roger's place. I found the Koba file . . ."

"You did?"

"Yeah, but the contents were missing. Did you take it?"

"Koba must have taken it," said the voice.

"Who is he, Jack?"

"He's an agent who's gone berserk. I almost had him yesterday."

"Almost doesn't count," said Morris.

"He's good," the voice said admiringly. "The guy is a professional."

"Well shit!" Morris yelled. "Do you want to give him a fuckin' medal?"

"Morris, listen to me. You're next . . ."

He felt his body start to freeze. "Next for what?"

"You're next on his list of victims."

"What list?"

"I found his list, Morris. And you're next . . ."

Morris held up his hand. "Wait a second, Jack. What are you talking about? I mean, first you say how clever and professional he is and then you tell me he's dumb enough to keep a list."

"He is clever, Morris. But he's also obsessed. It's not a rational act to try to destroy your past by killing off everyone you knew. This man is out to obliterate his history. He might know I'm onto him, but he's not to be deterred. On the other hand, that's our advantage. That's how we know we've got him!"

Morris got up and began pacing the room. Suddenly he stopped and held out his hand. "Give me a cigarette," he said.

"Look in your shirt," said the voice.

Drawing a smoke from his shirt pocket, Morris lit up. He took a puff and began pacing again. "What do you want me to do?" he asked.

"All I want you to do is act as bait. I'll do the rest."

Morris stared at the flowers in disbelief. "What are you talking about? You want me to be your sacrificial lamb?"

"No, Morris. Sacrificial is the wrong word. I want you to be the honey for the bear trap."

"You must think I'm incredibly dumb!" he said, mashing his cigarette into an empty plate.

"We're helping each other, Morris. You want your life. I want Koba. It's as simple as that."

"Why do you want Koba, Jack?" Morris looked at the flowers suspiciously. "What's he done to you?" He felt his anger start to grow. "Why have you been lying to me?"

"Very shortly you'll know all," said the voice.

"But why the hell should I trust you?"

It had a patronizing tone as it spoke. "Morris, do you know what it's like to be a hunted man? It plays on your imagination. Shadows haunt you at night and strange eyes watch you in the day. You might run away, but you'll never be able to turn a corner without seeing Koba's face. You might last a year or two, but finally he'll get you. And if he doesn't then the fear of him will. It's a fear that grows on you, Morris. It's like a cancer. It grows until it takes over your body and your mind. The asylums are full of people like you. They're filled to overflowing with people like you!"

Morris looked at the daisies and petunias and applauded. "Bravo! Bravo! Great speech, Jack! You've got a theatrical career in store for you when you finally quit the secret police!"

"Smug asshole! I don't know why I waste my time!" Suddenly the voice caught itself and grew calm again. "If you can't think of yourself, Morris, think of Heather and Rosa."

In a fury Morris reached for the milk bottle which held the bouquet and smashed it against the wall. He thrust his fingers at the scattered flowers. "Don't speak of them, you hear me! I never want to hear you utter their names again!"

Through the static he could hear the voice whisper. "Think of them, Morris. Think of them . . ."

The problem was that he had been thinking of them. And if what Jack was saying had any truth to it at all, their lives would be in peril too.

Morris sat back down. He felt exhausted. He looked at the mess on the floor. "What do you want me to do?" he said.

The voice was growing weaker, but Morris could hear it still: "Good, Morris, good. Just stay in your room tonight. Koba will come. But I'll be there as well. You might not see me at first, but I'll be there."

"How do you know he'll come?"

The voice was fading rapidly now. "He'll come, Morris. Trust me . . ."

And then with a final hiss, the voice expired.

Morris sat on his bed afterward, very still. He didn't feel like moving or thinking or sleeping. He just felt like being nothing: a cluster of molecules in space, without purpose, without reason; just there because it's there. And if a fly had come and landed on his nose, he probably wouldn't have bothered to brush it off.

But it's hard to be nothing for long. Muscles grow weary of sitting still. Backs start to ache. Nerves start to twitch. Thoughts begin to invade that precious vacuum in the mind. And so, even though he had no particular inclination, he got up.

The first thing he did was to sweep the floor. He got the broom form the corner where it stood precariously, always waiting to be knocked over, and began mechanically to sweep in long, steady motions, like an oarsman rowing down a river.

He swept all the flowers, all the petunias, marigolds, daisies and chrysanthemums into a pile along with the broken bits of glass and pushed them relentlessly toward the door. Opening it, he shoved them, with one quick flick of the broom, into the air.

He watched as the flowers, the bright reds and soft yellows, floated downward, dancing in the breeze, wafting back and forth in alternate currents of air, till they landed gently on the ground.

Then he grabbed his jacket and left.

He walked quickly down Valencia Street, across the flat, barren divide between the rich and the poor, past the soup kitchens and auto parts shops, past the scummy housing projects where young men lurked in dark shadows shooting hell into their veins, to Market Street.

Turning up Van Ness, he continued past City Hall with its classical rotunda and the marble auto mausoleums, so ghostly now, to California Street. At California he hopped onto a waiting cable car and rode it up to the top of the posh, to Nob Hill, where all the blood shed in angry demonstrations against the face of power and privilege had long since dried, and then down again, past the towering banks and majestic insurance companies and the offices of the high and mighty, to the foot of San Francisco: to the area that was once known as the Embarcadero, but now had become Rockefeller West, a self-contained village within the city, where brick cottages built atop the office blocks gave way to quiet brooks and tree-lined walks, leading to restaurants and boutiques all guarded twenty-four hours a day by an army of private security guards.

At the very end of the complex was the most lavish hotel in town — the Hyatt Regency. And it was to the Hyatt he had come. The hotel had been built several years before in a torrent of publicity. It was to be one of the great architectural wonders of the world. But as the structure grew, Morris had realized that he had seen its like before. Perhaps someplace in Mexico. It had the flavor of a hotel for Aztec millionaires.

He had visited it once before with Rosa, right after it had been built. Rosa had been intrigued by the place, which in her eyes looked very much like a lavish lean-to. Inside, in the large central lobby, however, they had been astounded by the fantasy world that had been created by the abundance of glass, concrete, and chrome molded into fountains and sunken bars and great translucent tubes, standing upright, which shot high into the sky.

Rosa had been awed by the magical fountain which held its waters so still one thought it might have been made of crystal. She had insisted on sticking her hand into the water to make sure it was real. It was. And so was the rushing brook that traversed the length of the open vestibule like a country stream. of course, she had to walk down the rocky path constructed alongside. And when she fell in, as he had known she would, he took her into the

160

men's toilet where she changed from her wet clothes into his undershirt which came down to her knees like a baggy mini-dress.

The downstairs bar had been transformed that afternoon into a dance spa. The chrome tables had been pushed up against the perimeter exposing the parquet squares. The music, bits of Viennese waltzes, came from the strings of tuxedoed musicians standing on white pedestals like mechanical statues dedicated to the memory of finer days when money and elegance went hand in hand. Days when someone like Morris would never have been allowed inside.

Morris was ushered to a vacant table by a waiter who wore finer clothes but escorted him with due respect, perhaps because he thought Morris to be one of those screwball tycoons that turned up every now and then.

The waiter bowed slightly. "What will you be ordering, sir?"

"I'm waiting for someone," said Morris. Suddenly he recognized the face. "Hey, aren't you Paul Brodsky? Remember me? We worked together down at local 10!"

The waiter looked perplexed. Then his eyes opened wide. "Morris?" he said. "Shit! What the fuck are you doing down here? You know what they charge for drinks in this dive?"

"You don't think I'd spend my dough in a place like this, do you? I'm waiting for a guy . . ."

"Oh," Brodsky winked. "I see."

"You don't see nothin'," said Morris. "I'm meeting my lawyer."

"Sure," said Brodsky. "What's his name so's I can send him to you?"

"His name is Bubbles. You'll know him 'cause he'll be wearing a pink wig and a sequined gown."

Brodsky shrugged his shoulders. "That's nothin' to me, Morris," he said. "I've seen 'em come, I've seen 'em go." And with that he walked away.

It was a strange assortment of types who had come to dance that afternoon. There were the older ladies and gentlemen, the ones who had probably gone tea dancing in their youth. They looked like they belonged. The younger ones seemed to have trouble with the beat, sliding over the floor in a distorted two-step. Some tried the tango; others, more modern dances. It created a bizarre image, as if someone had constructed a montage of photos taken in the same room over twenty-year increments.

Morris watched, intrigued, and he suddenly imagined himself waltzing there with Heather. She looked more beautiful and radiant than he had ever remembered. And as they danced, barely touching the floor, they drifted from the bar through the lobby and on out the door, up to their little town house overlooking the Bay, safely ensconced above the hustle and bustle, the dirt and the grime, the noise and pollution, the smelly drunks, the evil drugs, the worries of money, the tiresome chores, the threats of war, the sorrows of death, the pain and the suffering . . .

Caught up in this strange reverie, he suddenly noticed that Brodsky was hovering over him. Morris glanced up as Brodsky leaned down and winked. "Your lady friend, sir?"

Morris nodded. "Hello, Bubbles."

Rocky grimaced as he sat down at the table. He turned to the waiter. "Two Irish whiskies, straight up." And then, when Brodsky had gone, he said, "I can only stay a few minutes, Kaplan. But that's long enough to tell you what an ass you are."

"Did you bring the article?" asked Morris, ignoring Rocky's anger.

"Morris, there are some things in this world that are better off unknown."

"Not in my book."

The whiskies arrived. Brodsky, smirking, put them down before the two men and looking at Rocky, let out a low whistle.

"What's with him?" asked Rocky, pointing his thumb at the retreating waiter.

Morris shrugged and took out his crumpled pack of cigarettes, offering one to Rocky.

Rocky took a mangled smoke from the pack and stared at it. "Do you keep these in the back pocket of your pants?" he asked.

Striking a match, Morris held it out for Rocky to catch the flame. "A smoke's a smoke," he said.

Rocky stared at him for a moment. "I'm going to lay it on the line, Morris. I'm going to say it once and that's all. Not because it's going to do you any good, but because I owe you one."

"You owe me one?"

"Yes. Because of you, the mob decided to take their business elsewhere."

"You mean Bruno?"

Picking up his glass, Rocky bolted his drink straight down. Then he looked Morris in the eye and said, "Koba's dead, Morris."

"I don't believe you," Morris replied.

"He's dead," said Rocky, firmly. "But KOBA is alive."

Morris furrowed his brow. "I don't get you, Rocky. What are you saying."

"KOBA is a code word, Morris."

"For what?"

"For an independent supply line from Bolivia. It started out as an operation set up by Koba to help arm the guerrillas. Then something went wrong. Koba was caught and executed. But the network continued without interruption. Someone took it over."

"Were Roger and Philip involved?"

Rocky nodded. "Koba had set up his network with independent dealers in the States, small fry like Roger who had been active in the movement. He wanted to tap the market that always existed, the recreational users, the lefties, the beats, the hips — the ones who wouldn't mind seeing the profits used to help the revolution in South America."

"What was your role in this, Rocky?"

"I helped put him in contact with people like Roger. People who weren't mixed up with the organization."

"And then the thing started to fall apart, is that it?"

"You can't keep operations like that out of the hands of the pros, Morris. Their arms are too long."

"Who took over on the other end, Rocky? Who took Koba's place?"

Rocky shrugged. "I don't know. And frankly, I don't care." He looked at Morris with a solemn face. "These things have a way of devouring anyone who touches them. This isn't a game."

"I know. Roger is dead. Philip is dead. I may be next. Where's Roger's article, Rocky? Where's the file?"

"I've destroyed it, Morris."

Morris put his hand on his forehead and rubbed it for a moment. Then he looked up at Rocky, with pain in his eyes.

"This is the time to stop, Morris. Right now, before it's too late."

"That's exactly what I'm trying to do," said Morris, standing up to go. "I'm trying to stop it before it's too late."

Chapter Thirteen

He stopped at a pay–phone to call Heather.

"Oh, Moishe, thank heaven! Is Rosa with you?"

His confusion came through in his voice. "I got a message that you said she was staying with a friend!"

"She was supposed to but she never showed! Moishe, I'm so worried!"

"She came to see me yesterday, Heather. She was upset about you moving to Chicago . . ."

"You saw her!"

"We went down to Chinatown for a pork bun. She said she wanted to move in with me. I told her we'd have to talk it over with you. Then she ran away. I came back to the Meat Market and got your message, so I figured she was safe . . ."

"But where did she go?"

"I don't know." He hesitated for a moment. "Did you know that Roger was killed yesterday?"

"Roger Billings?"

"How many other Rogers do we know?"

"But he was at the wake! We were talking to him just the other day!"

"That was the day before he got shot."

"Who would shoot him, Moishe? Who would do such a thing?"

"Mary says he shot himself."

"He committed suicide? Roger?"

"That's what Mary says." There was silence on the other end. Then Morris said, "He was writing an article with Philip. It had something to do with the CIA. Rocky says that he and Philip were small-time dealers . . ."

"I don't want to hear any more, Moishe. I don't want to hear any of your conspiracy theories today."

"I think it has something to do with Koba, Heather. I think we're all in danger."

"Moishe! Please!" Her voice was pleading.

"Heather, did Puccini compose *La Bohème*?"

"What?"

"I think you ought to take Rosa and leave for a while. Go to Chicago . . ."

"You want me to take Rosa and leave? Well you go find her then!" she shouted.

He heard the receiver slam down at the other end of the line.

He took a bus along Market Street, up to Diamond Heights, alighting at the top of Clipper Hill. Below, the city was glowing through the mist, the tiny droplets distorting the light. The air had become dense, massy, leaden, like the somber weight that filled his head. He shuffled his feet. They felt swollen inside his shoes. His hands felt large and ungainly. His body was unresponsive; not light the way it was when he was young.

"Eyes that wouldn't see; ears that wouldn't hear." The words swirled in his mind like nonsense rhymes from the pen of Lewis Carroll.

"Free floating anxiety," Heather had once said.

"What? More psychology crap?" He had turned up his nose.

"It's what you call the tightness in your chest when you can't think of anything that's wrong."

He could think of lots that was wrong. There wasn't any end to it. But now he was consumed with thoughts of death and it made all the other things seem trivial.

Yet, when he considered it, his notion of death had become rather antiseptic. It was a death without remorse. A death without pity. An unheroic death. A senseless death.

Behind him, on the ocean side, the mist was hovering, straining to reach the top and spill over the sides of the hill down into the valley where the houses lay huddled, awaiting the bluster.

How would it be, he wondered? It was a childhood question. Would you run? Would you struggle? Would you go with dignity? Would you go like a hero, without a sign of emotion? Or would you shout, scream, bite, spit? Would you curse with every vile profanity you could muster? Or would your body go limp, like an empty vessel, a failed condom — defiled, degraded, contrite.

His anger began to grow as he walked down Clipper Hill. His muscles tightened. His fists clenched. "The function of the mind, the true function of the mind, is to circumvent death; to plan and avoid. To prepare for the final struggle. To be devious and cunning. There are no rules to the game. There are no friends, no comrades. Everyone is alone. Everyone is on their own."

He turned up Diamond Street. The chill air penetrated his bones. The heat of his growing anger fought it back. The fire was stoked within him like coals in a furnace. His face was flushed. He turned the corner. He opened the gate.

Arnold's garden sat quietly in the evening mist. The tender sprouts were moist. The vines clung to their trellis. The stalks of corn had begun to thicken — silk strands had penetrated the miniature husks. The tops of carrots, onions, radishes, and other edibles stood straight in their proper rows, like proud soldiers on parade.

Suddenly Morris found himself hating their arrogance. He hated the earth, the soil, the burial sites for human life returned in other forms. Returned as green vegetables! He thought of Roger. Perhaps he was a string-bean now. And Philip? An onion, he supposed. The thought was too much to endure. He began pulling at the carrots and the beans, hurling them in the air. He lunged at the corn and beat it down. He kicked at the radishes. He plundered the onions. It was done in fury. Vegetables were flung here and there, littering the fence and the pathway with their limp corpses.

The bulk of them lay in a pile, like the beginnings of a funeral pyre. They garnished the air with the stench of herbal decay. He looked at them without sympathy. Strangely, though, he felt better, as if a weight had been lifted from him in one enormous orgasm.

When it was over, he sat down in the wasted fields overlooking Arnold's house. His mind was clearer than it had been for days. His body was light again. He felt a sense of euphoria.

167

And then he got up from the ground, up from Arnold's former farm, now a graveyard. Somehow, he knew with certainty what he had to do. Without a moment's hesitation he went across the garden to the main house. The door was locked, but he knew that Arnold kept the key underneath the mat. He reached down, took it, and unlocked the door. He walked inside, straight up to Arnold's bedroom.

Arnold's shotgun lay by his bed. Morris took off his shoes and walked brazenly up to where Arnold was asleep, snoring away till the crack of dawn when once again he would do his postal rounds. Morris took the weapon and silently carried it out, back into the garden and on up the cottage stairs.

Inside the room he checked the chamber for ammunition and, seeing it was loaded, he snapped it shut again. Then he set it carefully on his bed while he began rummaging around for his old toolbox. He found it rusting away under the sink. But everything he needed was still there: hammer, nails, some plumbing tape, metal brackets, screws and such. He emptied it all in a heap onto the floor and immediately got down to work hammering in the braces. Then he took the shotgun and mounted it on top of his chest of drawers so that the muzzle faced the center of the room. After it was secured, he got out a piece of translucent nylon fishing line, fixing one end to the trigger mechanism and then running the rest down through a series of leads made from tiny bent nails. At the other end of the line he made a loop just large enough for his index finger. When he had finished, when the line was taut and the shotgun primed and cocked, he carefully placed a blanket over the entire apparatus and moved a straight-back chair alongside.

As soon as he sat down, he began to feel the fatigue. In a while, his body started to slump and he drifted off to sleep.

It was almost midnight when the knock finally came. Morris first heard it in his sleep and then, as it grew more insistent, he shook himself awake.

"Come in!" he shouted hoarsely. "The door's open!"

And then he remembered. The string! He reached for it, but, because it was translucent and blended so well with the surroundings, he couldn't find it. He swung his hand back and forth in a swatting motion, furiously searching for the elusive loop. But it was too late. For the door had now opened and a figure moved in from the darkness, out of the night.

"Hello, Jack," said Morris. His hand had ceased swinging.

Jack was wearing his trench-coat and hat as he stepped into the room. He smiled. "Hello, Morris."

"Did you bring a bottle?" he asked. "Or just your gun?"

"I'm sorry, Morris. But I won't be staying long." He motioned toward the chair that Morris had arranged for him. "May I sit down?"

"Yes," Morris replied without hesitation.

"I'm sorry I'm late," said Jack.

Morris shrugged.

"So you know why I'm here?" Jack stared at him strangely and Morris felt an unpleasant sensation in his spine. He knew now where he had seen that look before. It was just a few days ago — an eternity now — outside La Bohème.

"I think so," said Morris.

"Then who am I, Morris? You like playing guessing games, don't you? Who am I?"

"You're Jack Chesterton. A lying sonofabitch!"

"Well, you're partly right, Morris." He laughed. "Poor Morris. Always partly right."

It was the smile that annoyed him the most. That damn contemptuous smile!

"Don't worry," Jack went on, still staring directly into his eyes. "I'll tell you what you want to know. After all, I wouldn't want you to die of curiosity."

"Thanks," said Morris, furtively reaching once more for the string.

Jack crossed his legs and took up a story-telling position, leaning forward a bit. His face grew serious as he began to speak: "There was once a brilliant revolutionary, Morris — a North American who had the guts to forge links with the Bolivian guerrillas and to set up a network that put liberal American money into guerilla coffers.

"Of course, once the Company had identified him, it was certain he'd be caught. And when the thousands of dollars in

169

bribes paid off and he was finally captured, it was left to a young Company officer who had been recently stationed there to interrogate him.

"So the day after the capture a meeting was arranged with the Chief of Police. It was a very matter-of-fact meeting, simply a formality, you understand, to establish priority interest in this matter.

"As it happened, however, the meeting was held at the same time the locals had chosen to 'extract' their own information from the prisoner. The interrogation was being held in an adjoining room and the sounds soon penetrated the walls of the office where the Chief of Police and the Company officer were toasting their successful operation.

"Of course, the Chief of Police was very apologetic. According to protocol any torturing was to be done outside the presence of Company men. An attempt was made to mask the sounds by turning up the radio. But the noise was too strong to suppress. And finally the Chief of Police excused himself and went into the next room to demand quiet.

"However, by that time the Company officer had been quite shaken. You see, even though he had been an operative for a few years, he had never personally witnessed a torture session. And it terrified him.

"When the Chief of Police returned he offered to allow the Company officer to interview the American then and there, for it was no longer clear whether the American would last the night. The prisoner had been tougher than they expected and it had been necessary to use a great deal of persuasion to get him to talk. He was still conscious, but some vital organs had been damaged in the process of interrogation.

"The Company officer, therefore, was ushered into the numberless room next door. The guards, as instructed, took their leave. The metal door clanged shut and the Company officer was left alone with the prisoner."

Jack stopped his monologue for a moment. Morris sensed a different look about him, as if Jack, himself, was undergoing a transformation.

"It had been bright in the hallway and it took a moment for the

170

Company officer's eyes to adjust to the relative darkness of the cell. At first, all he perceived was a strange and powerful odor. It was a smell he had never sensed before. It was animalistic and primal. It was disgusting, even horrifying, but at the same time it had a strange sensual quality to it. And it triggered in him a very intense and curious emotion.

"The cell itself was tiny, built out of damp and musty rock. The periphery of the room was dark. Just a single dim light bulb dangled from the center of the ceiling. And under that light, manacled to chains which hung from opposite walls, was the American. He was naked and covered with blood which was caked to his body in brownish lumps. His eyes were opened wide, gazing up, like two brilliant candles, toward the ceiling. And his arms, because of the manacles, were stretched as far as they could go, as were his legs.

"As he stood there in the shadows, by the door of the cell, the Company officer, who had never been a religious man, couldn't help but think about the first time he had been brought to church as a young boy and had witnessed the frightening crucifixion statues, with those horribly sensual welts of blood painted in crimson on sinewy arms, those eyes uplifted in sublime agony, and that faint smile of terrible pain and understanding and . . . forgiveness."

"Was the American alive?" asked Morris, his voice shaking slightly.

The voice from across the room had softened in reverence. "Yes, he was alive. Yet he was no longer of mortal flesh. He was in a certain state of grace. For the American had attained a power which few can comprehend. Certainly not you, Morris. But in that moment of witness, the Company officer understood. And he fell to his knees faintly dizzy and struggling for breath.

"How long he knelt there, before the American, I don't remember. It really doesn't matter. But soon he became aware that the light overhead had been magnified a thousandfold and in its place was a glow so sweet and bright and pure that his miserable body, once gasping for air, felt free and supple and, strangely enough, he was overcome with a feeling of sublime joy.

"This transformation may have taken place in a matter of

171

moments, but for the Company officer it was as if centuries of wisdom had been compressed into seconds. And when he rose to his feet he was no longer the same. Nor would he ever be the same again.

"He spent that afternoon interviewing the American, though 'interview' is hardly the right word. What he wanted, what he needed, was a history. In that short time, he made a record of the American's life. For, by then, he knew that he had been chosen for that one purpose, like the prophets of old. And he knew, that in some strange way, by some divine guidance, all his training had brought him to this very room. And all the years of learning, the years of experience in gathering information, quickly, precisely, accurately, were now to be put to service for his true life's work."

Jack suddenly stopped. Then he said, "Are you beginning to understand, Morris."

Morris nodded slowly. "The American — he was Koba?"

"Yes."

"And he died that evening?"

"His mortal body. Yes."

"And the Company officer?"

"That was my former self."

"And now . . ." He found it difficult to say. "Now you've become Koba."

"I have taken on the name and mantle, Morris. You see, Jack died in that cell along with Koba. Only Koba was resurrected. Like the phoenix, Koba could not be destroyed. He would rise up again, stronger than before."

"But why are you here?" said Morris, hardly daring to ask.

"At first, Morris, I thought I could use you. I thought you could help me tell the world of Koba and His Coming. But now I realize how absurd that was."

The figure stared across the room at the bearded man with the terrified eyes. "You disgust me, Morris. You are not worthy to be one of His Prophets!"

Morris felt his heart reach his throat, but he found enough strength to speak. "Koba was a dope dealer! How the hell can you deify him?"

Suddenly the figure rose and pointed a menacing finger. "You sniveling moron! You play with mindless rhetoric and then call yourself a revolutionary! To you, the height of militancy is a brick through a window. And when in your stupid ineptitude you get caught, you burst into tears when your wrist gets slapped! You know nothing of the struggle, the life-and-death struggle for change. Koba knew. He knew that force can only be challenged by force. That violence can only be challenged by greater violence. Revolution is not a child's game. It's mean and cruel and dirty. To you, Morris, it's just a stupid dream of green fields and barefoot children. You use catchwords like 'peace' and 'justice' without knowing what they mean or having any idea how to attain them. And for fools like you, that's all it can ever become. Just a dream. But Koba was different. He knew that in the process of cleaning the gutter you can't avoid the slime. You and your friends were never worthy to lick his boots!"

"And you?" Morris shouted back. "Who are you? A filthy agent of the secret police! Your heart bleeds for Koba since he was a victim you saw in the flesh! How about the thousands you didn't see?"

"And if they died for the revolution, they need not have died in vain!"

"Like the old woman you killed in front of La Bohème? Did she die for the revolution as well?"

"Yes. It was necessary to kill her to see if you could stand the test . . ."

"The test? What test?"

"The test of blood, Morris. The test of fire. And you failed, Morris. You failed miserably. You're nothing but a whining child. You're not fit to be a soldier of the revolution!"

"Whose revolution?" Morris shouted. "Your revolution? Koba's revolution? Certainly not my revolution! I was fighting for a more humane world! You think you can work to destroy us for all these years and then call yourself a revolutionary just because you changed your hat? Just who the hell do you think you are, you crazy bastard!"

"I am Koba! I am Koba the magnificent! I am the creator and destroyer of all worlds! I am the Revolution!"

And with that he pulled a revolver from his pocket, pointing it directly at Morris' head. His voice softened as he spoke. "Morris, the time has come . . ."

"For what?" asked Morris in a trembling voice, his finger reaching for the elusive string. "You're not going to shoot me are you, Jack? We were buddies, remember?"

"Not yet, Morris. Not yet. I want you to suffer first. Before you go, I want you to know that all is lost. There is no hope for you and your kind. No hope at all."

Morris kept his hand swinging, feeling for the invisible wire. "I don't have any hope, Jack. Honestly. None at all."

"Rosa's dead, Morris." He smiled.

Morris' hand stopped in mid-air.

"What?"

"Rosa's dead. I killed her."

"I don't believe you," he said. The blood had drained from his face. "You've lied to me before. You've never stopped lying. You're just a fucking liar, Jack! She's alive!"

"No, Morris. She's dead. You have nothing left to live for. Nothing at all."

"Rosa's alive! You're a raving loony, Jack. You're going to be put in a padded cell!"

The figure took a cap from his pocket and tossed it to Morris. It landed in his lap. "Remember, Morris. You said she looked like a *Dead End* kid in it. I bugged you, Morris. I heard everything you said this past week!"

Morris looked down at his lap. Slowly his fingers touched the cloth, as if it were a sleeping baby. He lifted it gently and put it to his face. He kissed it. The tears flowed from his eyes.

"You're not dead Rosa, honey. You're not dead. Remember, I taught you how to fly! Don't you remember sweetheart? I said to think real hard and concentrate on your arms and then you just feel the feathers start to grow. 'Think', I told you. 'Think you're a bird.' And then, just when the witch is about to turn you into a chocolate chip cookie, you start to flap your wings as fast and as hard as you can!"

"What the hell are you doing, Morris? You think your fantasy games will get you out of this one?"

"Just flap them hard. And believe, Rosa, baby! You're not dead! I know! You flew away and your hat fell from your head."

"Stop it, Morris!" Koba took aim.

His arms were flapping as hard as they could. He could feel the feathers start to sprout. The wind from his wings was enormous. Papers began to rustle and then scatter from his desk.

"Now fly, Rosa! Fly!"

His finger hit the invisible string. The blast shattered through the room. The heat was red, then white. The celluloid began to burn. The picture faded out.

Chapter Fourteen

She opened the door and saw him standing there. His face was white. His eyes were glazed.

"Moishe!" she said. "Where have you been? I've been trying to call you! Your phone must still be out of order!"

He was standing in the doorway. Mute. She threw herself into his arms. "She hasn't come back! I don't know where she could be!"

She felt his body, limp, against hers. She let go of him and stood back a pace.

He went inside and collapsed onto the settee. He held his head in his hands.

She closed the front door and went over to where he was sitting. He looked up at her. She had never seen his face like that before.

She knelt down and took his hand. "Moishe. You're crying."

He closed his eyes. She sat down next to him and held him in her arms.

"Shhh, Moishe. She'll be all right. I know she'll be all right."

She felt his tears on her hands.

"The police were here. They said it was too soon to worry."

He shook his head. "You don't understand, Heather . . ."

"What don't I understand?"

He looked at her. It was a pitiful look. He reached in his pocket and took out the hat.

"Where did you get that?" she asked.

"It was hers."

"No, Moishe. It's mine."

"I know. She found it in the closet. I told her she needed a hat."

"When was that?"

"Does it matter?" He took her in his arms. "Oh, Heather! What have I done?"

"What have you done, Moishe? What are you trying to say?"

"Our little girl . . ."

Suddenly Heather began to pick up on his emotion. "Is there something I don't know?" She pulled away from him. "Moishe! Tell me!"

Just then there was a thudding at the door.

He stood up. "It's the cops!" he said. He looked at her sitting there. "Heather," he said, "Rosa's dead."

She stared at him uncomprehendingly. "What?"

The tears streamed from his eyes. "Rosa is dead!"

The thudding at the door became more intent.

Heather got up, mechanically, and walked over to the front door.

At first he felt the blood draining from his head. Then he felt the ground give way. He fell to the floor in a heap.

"Rosa!" he shouted, bolting upright in the bed.

"It's all right, Moishe." Heather was sitting next to him, sponging his head with cool water. "She's fine. Curly, your friend from the docks, brought her home. He found her yesterday roaming around, down by Aquatic Park. She wouldn't tell him where she lived until late last night. It was Curly who was knocking at the door when you collapsed, not the cops."

He clutched her hand. "She's not dead?"

"Of course not, Moishe! I told you she'd be OK. She knows how to take care of herself. And that's more than I can say for you. Arnold, your landlord, phoned me an hour ago. He said he heard an explosion coming from the cottage sometime after midnight. When he got there he found his shotgun bolted to your chest of drawers and a great big hole in the wall . . ."

"That's all? Just a hole in the wall?"

"He also said his garden was raped, pillaged and plundered by someone."

"He didn't find a body on the floor?"

She looked at him with some concern. "What happened, Moishe?"

177

"Heather," he said, "I killed someone."

"Who?"

"Koba."

She sighed. "And the body just disappeared. Like Leon the kangaroo."

"I didn't kill Leon," he said.

She shook her head like a mother hearing a confession from a naughty boy. "Arnold says he's through with you, Moishe. He says he doesn't want to be a beastly landlord, but shooting holes in the wall is forbidden in the lease."

"He's evicting me?" asked Morris, raising his eyebrows.

"Half the city is being evicted, Moishe. And not even for shooting holes in their walls."

He looked into her eyes. "Heather," he said calmly, "it wasn't a hallucination."

She smiled. "Go back to sleep, Moishe. We'll talk about it over breakfast."

He got up and grabbed his clothes.

"Where are you going?" she asked.

"I'll be back," he said. "I just need some air."

He walked to Fredo's place with wobbly legs. It was like walking in a dream. But Heather thought the dream had been last night. He couldn't convince her that Koba was dead.

As he banged on Fredo's window, he began to feel the panic surge in him again. Arnold had found the rifle bolted to the chest of drawers. He had heard the blast and seen the hole. But what happened to the body? What happened to the blood?

The door finally opened and there stood Fredo, reassuringly disheveled and unkempt. He almost felt like hugging his old friend, if Fredo had been the huggable sort.

"Where the hell have you been?" asked Fredo, ushering him inside. "I've been trying to get a hold of you since yesterday. Something must be wrong with your goddamn phone again!"

Morris shoved some papers aside and sank down into Fredo's couch. "I've been inside the eye of a nightmare," he said. And

178

then, noticing that his friend was busily throwing odds and ends into an old leather suitcase, he added, "What's up, Fredo? You going somewhere?"

Fredo looked at him with wild eyes and let out a croaking sort of laugh. "Damn right! I'm getting my ass out of here! Aren't you?"

"What are you talking about, Fredo?"

"What am I talking about?" Fredo stared at him as if he were mad. "What am I talking about? You were the one who was yapping about saving my bloody neck!"

Morris rubbed the side of his face, by the temple, hoping the throbbing ache would go away. "Fredo . . ."

Throwing in another pair of trousers that he found under a chair, Fredo muttered, "Don't try to tell me you were hallucinating again, Morris. Don't give me any Leon the kangaroo crap!"

Morris shook his head. "I don't know. I just don't know. Maybe I was hallucinating . . ."

Fredo glared at him fiercely. "What the hell are you jabbering on about, Morris? Were Philip and Roger hallucinations, too?"

"No, but . . ."

"No but what? I suppose that call I got last night was a hallucination as well?"

Morris stared at him curiously. "What call?"

"The call from Koba, damn it!" he shouted, throwing a package of half-eaten potato-chips into the suitcase and slamming it shut.

The throbbing was getting more intense. "Calm down," said Morris, as much to himself as to his friend. "When did you get this call?"

"I don't know," said Fredo, closing the latch. "Late last night . . ."

"What did he say?"

Fredo took off his belt and wrapped it around the valise. "Just that he wanted to see me."

"Just that?"

Fredo sat down on top of his possessions and put his head in his hands. "Yeah. Just that." He looked up at Morris. His expression was almost pitiful. "But I know it was him . . ."

"How do you know it was him, Fredo?"

"I heard him whisper his name. I'm sure I did!"

Morris sighed. "Fredo, Koba is dead. I killed him. I shot him last night."

Fredo shook his head. His eyes were blazing. "You're wrong, Morris! Koba is alive!"

"Do you remember our conversation the other day when I was so upset?" Morris said. "Remember when you told me that I needed facts to come to an intelligent conclusion about things? Well, you were right."

"Remember when you said that there're other ways of understanding? Well, you were right!" Fredo shot back.

"Fredo, paranoia is like cancer. If you don't cut it out it takes over your entire system. Believe me, I know."

"Tell that to Philip and Roger." With a pleading tone in his voice he said, "Morris, they're out to get us. I thought about it all last night. I didn't sleep a wink."

"Listen to me, Fredo. Last night I killed Koba. I shot him."

"I thought you said it was a hallucination."

"It wasn't a hallucination. I shot him. He's dead."

Fredo rubbed his curly hair with a nervous hand. "Morris, even if you did shoot him, how do you know he was dead?"

"Because I saw the body. I saw the blood. I saw the hole I shot through him. I know he was dead."

"Did a doctor sign a death certificate?"

"No . . ."

"Where's the body now?"

"I don't know." Morris sighed. "Arnold said there wasn't any body . . ."

Fredo got up and grabbed his suitcase.

"I'm not crazy Fredo. I swear to you. I shot him. I know he's dead!"

"Maybe you shot him. And maybe the CIA came with their cleaning crew and cleaned up the place ten minutes later." He stared into his eyes. "Morris, you were right all along. Koba killed Philip and Roger and now he's after us. I stayed up thinking about it all last night and I decided that it's precisely what happens when revolutions are in retreat. They just pick us off one by one. They can call it random murder or suicide or cancer or anything they want. But those buggers know what they're doing. They just wait till we fall apart and then they take their revenge!"

"But think about it, Fredo. We're no threat to them now."

Fredo shook his head. "Maybe not now. But we might be in the future. Morris, don't you understand? They want to wipe out the past so there can't be a future!"

Morris looked up compassionately at his old friend. "Maybe what we're feeling is our own mortality, Fredo. Maybe what died is our youth and some of our ideals. But the secret police aren't phantoms. When we give them that kind of power we're just doing their job for them. And when that happens we might just as well give up the ship."

Fredo shrugged and grabbed his valise. "Well, Morris," he said, "maybe you're right and maybe you're not. But I ain't waiting around to find out. You remember the old mole?"

"The old mole?"

"Yeah," said Fredo, "the old mole. One of Lenin's little pets. Instead of staying like a martyr and being nailed to the garden gate, he decided to live underground, preparing his strategy and waiting to fight another day."

Morris watched his friend walk over and open up the door. "Where are you going to go? Or shouldn't I ask?"

Suddenly a sly smile appeared on Fredo's face. "With the Basque," he said.

"You mean the waitress from the Café Picaro?"

"Yeah. She and I are headed for southern France. She's got a bungalow somewhere near Carcassonne. There's room for one more if you want to come."

Morris shook his head. "I'm not much into *ménages á trois*."

Fredo shrugged. "Well — see you around, I guess."

"Yeah, see you around."

"Don't bother locking up. I've left a few surprises for the chiropractor and I wouldn't want to make it hard for him to find them. Don't touch any wires."

Morris nodded.

And with one of those final movements one might have seen in an old '40s film, Fredo pushed back his Irish worker's cap in a jaunty sort of way, winked his eye and left.

The morning mist still shrouded yesterday's battlefield as Morris made his way back through the garden gate. Arnold's farm was a mess. It looked like the end result of a poorly planned demolition project.

Morris climbed up the rickety steps and opened his front door. He stayed at the entrance a moment, surveying the scene. There was hardly anything different about it, except the hole in the wall. Even the contraption he had built to mount Arnold's rifle had been carefully dismantled.

He walked inside and looked around. There had to be some evidence, he thought, no matter how minute, how small, which could prove he wasn't mad.

He got down on his hands and knees and began to examine the floor. Whoever had taken the body away and cleaned up must have done so very fast. They couldn't have accounted for everything. He was searching for some sign, some inkling, that last night's drama had, indeed, been real.

And then, in the corner of the room, he found it. Or, at least, he thought he did. They were two tiny spots of brownish stuff which the cleaning crew had missed. He went to his desk and got his penknife and a tiny plastic bag which had held some rubber bands. He got down on his hands and knees again and carefully scraped the spots from the floor. Placing the evidence in the plastic bag, he went back to his desk, taped it shut, and put the tiny receptacle into the pocket of his jacket.

Chapter Fifteen

Heather answered the door. "Good," she said, "you're back! Have a nice walk?"

"Productive," he said, coming inside.

"Well, you're just in time . . ." she began, as she led the way to the kitchen.

"In time for what?"

"Rosa's making breakfast for us. Sort of as a celebration."

"A celebration?"

"Yeah. Today's the day."

"The day. What day?"

"Don't you remember? Well, it figures . . ." She shook her head.

Rosa was standing by the stove making flapjacks. She turned around and gave him a radiant smile. "Hi, Moishe," she said. "Sorry about last night."

He went over to where she was standing and picked her up and squeezed her as tight as he could.

"Hey, Moishe! You're hugging a little too hard, you know. Maybe you better put me down before the flapjacks burn, OK?"

"Sure, Rosa," he said. And he put her down again.

"Look what Heather got!" she said, pointing with her spatula to the table.

There were three large styrofoam cups by each place setting. "A double espresso for you, Moishe. A cappuccino for Heather. And a *caffelatte* for me! How's that? All together again for the celebration!"

"What celebration?" asked Morris, looking over at Heather. "I'm sorry, whatever it is, I've forgotten."

Heather smiled and picked up her pocketbook. "It's the changing of the guard, Moishe," she said, getting out her set of keys and tossing them to him. "My year is up. It's your turn."

"My turn for what?" He looked at Rosa.

"To play Daddy!" she said with grin.

He turned back to Heather. "Where are you going?"

"Well, first off, I'm quitting my job," she said, ticking the list on her fingers. "Then second, I'm moving into Mary's . . ."

"Mary's?" Morris gasped.

"Just till I find a place of my own. And, third, I'm getting involved again. I'm a good organizer, Moishe. I'm a lot better at that than I am as a prison guard."

"I tried to tell you, Heather."

"Well, you were right, Moishe. And now you'll have a chance to prove how right you are. All you have to do is feed her, clothe her, send her to school and pay the rent. It shouldn't be too hard."

He rubbed his head. "You sure you can't stay, Heather?"

"I thought about it, Moishe. Really I did. But it's better this way."

"Well, why don't you keep a key. Just in case . . ."

She smiled. "Leave Rosa's window unlocked some night. Maybe you'll have a surprise visitor."

It was late the same day when Morris and Rosa walked up 24th Street toward the Meat Market Café.

"You got any dough?" he asked her as they neared the door.

"Fifty cents," she said. "Heather gave me a dollar allowance every week. How much do you give?"

He muttered something that she couldn't hear. Searching in his pocket, he realized he hadn't any change. "Maybe Larry will put it on the tab," he said.

But when they reached the café they found that the door was bolted shut.

"Hey, Moishe, it's dark inside," said Rosa, putting her nose against the glass.

"Maybe Curtis forgot to pay the electricity bill," said Morris, rattling the door.

"Maybe it's a holiday," she suggested.

"Cafés do their best business on holidays, Rosa," he said. "Besides, it's not a holiday." He gave her a look. "How come you're not at school?"

"It's a celebration, remember?"

He groaned. And then he saw the sign.

"Closed until further notice due to governmental greed."

"What does that mean?" she asked, when he pointed the sign out to her.

Morris let out a sigh. "It means Curtis didn't pay his taxes and that I'll have to look for another office."

"Poor Moishe," she said as they walked on up the street, toward the park.

He gave her a wink. "Don't worry, Rosa. It's not that easy to keep us down."

"So what are we gonna do?"

"First thing we do is get a newspaper," he said.

Fortunately, a young man had just purchased a newspaper from a vending machine and politely held it open as Morris ran over and retrieved a free one.

"See?" he said, coming back with the paper tucked under his arm. "Things are looking up already!"

The sun was warm. Morris took off his jacket and flung it over his shoulder.

"But what are we going to do about an office?" asked Rosa, giving him a questioning look.

"We'll have to find temporary quarters," he said.

"Where?" she asked.

He pointed across the green. "See that bench?"

"You mean that's gonna be our office?"

He shrugged. "Well, just temporarily until they open the Meat Market again."

"What if they never open it again?"

"Never say never," he said.

They walked across the large expanse of green where children played and settled themselves on the wooden bench. Morris took his paper and opened it up.

"Can I have part?" asked Rosa.

"Sure. What do you want? Comics or sports?"

She pointed to the headlines. "Hey, wasn't Rocky Calhoon one of the guys in our casebook?" she asked.

Morris glanced where she was pointing. "You're right, Rosa. He sure as hell was!"

"What's it say about him, Moishe?"

He read the article aloud: "'Rocky Calhoon, the well-known attorney who has defended many of the city's radical causes over the last decade, was arrested last night for possession of narcotics. Lieutenant Brian Murphy, who is in charge of the investigation, said that Mr Calhoon is suspected of heading a drug ring responsible for bringing in much of the cocaine that has been flooding the city over the last year. Mr Calhoon, who denied the charge, is being defended by his father, Seamus Calhoon, known in the city's labor movement as 'The Fighting Irishman'.'"

"You think he's guilty?" she asked.

"If he is, there's a lot of people who are guiltier."

"But he shouldn't have been flooding the city with cocaine. That's not a very nice thing to do," she said.

"Rocky once told me that people get busted for what they didn't do, not for what they did."

"So you think it was a bum rap?"

"It's just part of a very complex story."

"I still don't understand what it's about, Moishe . . .'

"I told you before. It has to do with drugs and guns and revolution. Anyway, you're much too young to understand."

"Oh, come on, Moishe. Try me!"

He sighed. "Well, there was this guy we used to know who wanted to help the revolutionaries in Bolivia. He saw that they were very poor and didn't have much money to buy guns. But he also noticed that they had access to stuff that a lot of people back in the States wanted pretty bad . . ."

"Cocaine?"

"Yeah, cocaine. So he set up a supply network with people who were sympathetic to his cause. He shipped them cocaine and then used the profits to buy weapons and supplies for the guerrillas who were fighting the government . . ."

"I thought you didn't like people using those kind of drugs, Moishe."

186

"It doesn't matter what I think, Rosa. The fact is a good number of people from all political persuasions use them. And countries like Bolivia supply them. To the farmers there it's just another product, like corn or peanuts. It's just that the market for cocaine brings in a lot more cash."

"Anyway, how does all this relate to Koba?" she asked.

"We're getting to that," he said. "You see, the drug trade in South America has been going on for a long time and as long as the profits were being used to prop up dictatorships, the main suppliers weren't tampered with . . ."

"I thought the government tried to send drug pushers to jail," Rosa interjected.

"Just the small fry, Rosa. Like Curly said, it's a big business. In fact, as Roger and Philip discovered, agencies like the CIA have an interest in keeping the supply lines functioning — as long as people who support them are involved. But when independent dealers start getting involved, then they don't like it at all. And when people like Koba try using those massive profits to help support the guerrillas, they get very angry indeed."

"Wait a second. I thought Koba was the guy who was trying to kill you!"

"Koba wasn't only a person, Rosa. Koba was also a code name for the cocaine network set up to help the guerrillas."

"So what happened?"

"What happened is someone from the CIA, a Company officer named Jack, found out about Koba and took it over . . ."

"And Jack became Koba?"

"Right. You see, Roger and Philip found out that something was up."

"How'd they do that?"

"They were journalists who were scratching for a living and supplementing their income with a little dealing — in fact they were part of the KOBA connection. One day they must have realized that someone else had taken over on Koba's end, while on Rocky's end the mob was trying to muscle their way in. They suspected the CIA and decided to blow the whistle on the whole operation."

"But that meant blowing the whistle on themselves, didn't it, Moishe?"

"Maybe it did. But in the end they were true radical journalists. Someone like Roger couldn't pass up a great story, especially if it meant exposing a link between the mob and the CIA! The only problem is that they didn't realize Koba was a loony."

"But why was Koba after you?"

"Because he must have figured I was on to him as well."

"You think Koba's still out to get you?"

"Not anymore. I killed him last night."

Her eyes grew wide. "You did? How'd you do that, Moishe?"

"I blasted him with Arnold's rifle."

"Wow!"

"The only problem is that the body's missing."

"What do you think happened to it, Moishe?"

He shook his head. "Maybe the CIA didn't want his body found and too many embarrassing questions asked."

"Then how are you sure you killed him?"

"I saw him Rosa. I know when someone's dead."

She looked at him suspiciously. "How do you know it wasn't just one of your nightmares, Moishe? You've been having a lot of 'em these days."

"It wasn't a nightmare, Rosa."

"How do you know? I mean, if the body's missing . . ."

He smiled. "I've got some evidence," he said, reaching over and taking the jacket he had draped over the bench.

"What kind of evidence?"

"I found some blood spots in the room that they missed when they were cleaning up."

"What good does that do?" she asked.

"What good does that do? Why Rosa, once we take that blood to the laboratory, we can find out almost anything."

"Like what?"

"Like if the blood belonged to Koba. And if it did, then Koba was in my room. And if he was in my room, I damn well killed him!"

"But how can you tell if the blood belonged to Koba?"

"Rosa," he said, "that's one thing modern science can do. Give 'em a drop of blood and they can tell not only what you had for breakfast last Tuesday, but what color your kid's eyes will be."

"All that from a drop of blood?"

"Yep. From one drop of blood."

"Can I see?"

"See what?"

"The sample you scraped off the floor."

"Why? You can't tell anything till we bring it to the lab."

"Oh, come on, Moishe," she said excitedly. "Please! I just want to see!"

"OK," he said, reaching into his jacket pocket, "but you can only look. You can't touch."

He reached deep into his pocket, feeling all around.

"What's wrong, Moishe? Isn't it there?"

"It's there all right," he growled, turning the pocket inside out.

"Maybe there's a hole in it," she said, pointing to the pocket.

"There's no hole!" he snapped.

"You don't have to get angry," she said.

"Maybe it's another pocket," he said, turning them inside out, one by one.

"Moishe, you were carrying your jacket over your shoulder — remember? The pockets were upside down. Maybe it fell out."

He looked at her. "You're right, Rosa! That's what happened." He stared out at the long expanse of green they had walked through to get to the bench.

"You want to be an investigator?" he asked.

Her eyes lit up. "Sure, Moishe! You mean you and me?"

He nodded. "Yep. You and me. Moishe and daughter."

"Is that what it'll say on our card?"

"I'll phone the change in to Larry today."

"Great!" she said. "What's our first case?"

He got down on his hands and knees. "It's a tiny plastic bag, Rosa. I used to keep rubber bands in it. Now it's got two little scrapings of dried blood."

She got down next to him. "This is fun, Moishe!" she said. "It's almost like we were cows."

He started to crawl forward, brushing the grass with his fingers.

"What if we don't find it?" she called out.

"We'll find it, Rosa. Investigators never give up."

In the distance, the mist was hovering over the hills. Soon it would descend into the valley as it did every night. But now the sun was out and even though he was on his knees, Morris felt a breath of life.